THE ROYAL HOUSE OF NIROLI

Always passionate, always proud.

**The richest royal family in the world—
a family united by blood and passion,
torn apart by deceit and desire.**

More about Niroli...

The central part of the island is devoted mainly to the vineyards extending to the rolling foothills of the mountains. The Niroli vines produce the queen of white grapes. Cultivated since Roman times on the slopes of the Cattina Valley, and ripened by summer sun and storms, they are harvested to make a dry white wine that makes an especially good accompaniment to fish dishes.

There are also olive groves, orchards and the famous orange groves of Cattina. Oil of Niroli, extracted from the orange skins, has a floral, sweet and exotic scent. The oil has special healing, rejuvenating, soothing and restorative properties, making it especially popular for relaxation and antiaging treatments.

The volcanoes on Niroli are now extinct, but the area around them is still a rich source of volcanic mud. The Santa Fiera Spa specializes in volcanic-mud baths and masks as health and beauty treatments.

The Official Fierezza Family Tree

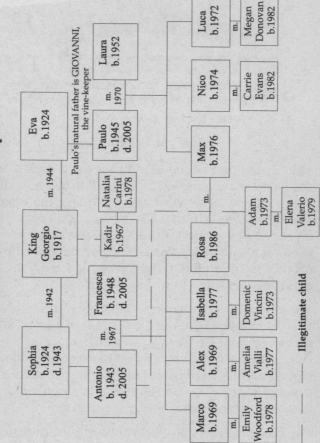

Paulo's natural father is GIOVANNI, the vine-keeper

Sophia b.1924 d.1943 — m. 1942 — King Georgio b.1917 — m.1944 — Eva b.1924

Antonio b.1943 d.2005 — m. 1967 — Francesca b.1948 d.2005

Paulo b.1945 d.2005 — m. 1970 — Laura b.1952

Kadir b.1967 — Natalia Carini b.1978

Maro b.1969 — m. — Emily Woodford b.1978

Alex b.1969 — m. — Amelia Vialli b.1977

Isabella b.1977 — m. — Domenic Vincini b.1973

Rosa b.1986 — m. — Max b.1976

Adam b.1973 — m. — Elena Valerio b.1979

Nico b.1974 — m. — Carrie Evans b.1982

Luca b.1972 — m. — Megan Donovan b.1982

— — — — — Illegitimate child

Penny Jordan
A ROYAL BRIDE AT THE SHEIKH'S COMMAND

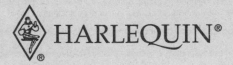

HARLEQUIN®

TORONTO • NEW YORK • LONDON
AMSTERDAM • PARIS • SYDNEY • HAMBURG
STOCKHOLM • ATHENS • TOKYO • MILAN • MADRID

ISBN-13: 978-0-373-12699-6
ISBN-10:   0-373-12699-9

A ROYAL BRIDE AT THE SHEIKH'S COMMAND

First North American Publication 2007.

Copyright © 2007 by Harlequin Books S.A.

Special thanks and acknowledgment are given to Penny Jordan for her contribution to THE ROYAL HOUSE OF NIROLI series.

www.eHarlequin.com

Printed in U.S.A.

The Rules

Rule 1: The ruler must be a moral leader. Any act that brings the Royal House into disrepute will rule a contender out of the succession to the throne.

Rule 2: No member of the Royal House may be joined in marriage without consent of the ruler. Any such union concluded results in exclusion and deprivation of honors and privileges.

Rule 3: No marriage is permitted if the interests of Niroli become compromised through the union.

Rule 4: It is not permitted for the ruler of Niroli to marry a person who has previously been divorced.

Rule 5: Marriage between members of the Royal House who are blood relations is forbidden.

Rule 6: The ruler directs the education of all members of the Royal House, even when the general care of the children belongs to their parents.

Rule 7: Without the approval or consent of the ruler, no member of the Royal House can make debts over the possibility of payment.

Rule 8: No member of the Royal House can accept an inheritance or any donation without the consent and approval of the ruler.

Rule 9: The ruler of Niroli must dedicate their life to the kingdom. Therefore they are not permitted to have a profession.

Rule 10: Members of the Royal House must reside in Niroli or in a country approved by the ruler. However, the ruler *must* reside in Niroli.

THE ROYAL HOUSE OF NIROLI
Always passionate, always proud.

Harlequin Presents is delighted to bring you the final instalment from THE ROYAL HOUSE OF NIROLI, in which you can follow the epic search for the true Nirolian king. Eight heirs, eight romances, eight fantastic stories!

The complete collection...

PROLOGUE

SHE was in total shock.

She needed very badly to sit down, but of course she couldn't. For one thing she was still in the Royal Presence Chamber, and, whilst she was a modern go-getting woman, her Nirolian ancestry within her reminded her that she was alone in the presence of Niroli's King.

And for another... Well, she told herself grimly, the king wasn't going to welcome seeing any kind of weakness being shown by the bride he had selected for this newly discovered heir. So newly discovered, in fact, that she, the bride-to-be in question, had been sworn to absolute secrecy about the whole thing.

It was of course a story that would attract every member of the paparazzi like blood in the water attracted sharks, and one that could be just as potentially perilous to anyone who obstructed King Giorgio's plans. She had just learned that these plans required her, as a dutiful subject, to marry this Prince Kadir Zafar, the King's previously 'secret' illegitimate son, for the sake of the island she loved so passionately.

CHAPTER ONE

Venice

SHE might be passionately attached to Niroli, but there was no doubt that Venice had a very special place in her heart, Natalia acknowledged, lifting her hand to try to stop the breeze from playing with the heavy weight of her thick dark curls. She was waiting for the water taxi to take her to her destination, and was totally oblivious to the admiring male looks she was attracting. When one man proved bold enough to murmur, *'Bella, bella,'* caressingly as he stopped to stand and stare openly at her, she couldn't help but laugh, her marine blue eyes sparkling with the rich colour of the lido in the sunshine. Just having her sombre mood lightened for a few seconds was a much needed relief at the moment.

It was all very well having sleepless nights and worrying herself half a stone thinner over whether or not she had made the right decision, but what she ought to be asking herself surely was why on earth had she ever agreed to do it in the first place.

The water taxi arrived and she picked up her small weekend bag and stepped into the taxi with ease and elegance. She was a tall woman of close to six feet who wore her height with calm pride.

'Via Venetii? The Buchesetti Spa Hotel,' she asked the *vaporetto* driver.

'*Sì*,' he agreed, with open admiration in his gaze.

The tranquil ride to her destination made Natalia reflect ruefully on the uncomfortable speed with which the direction of her life had suddenly changed. Increasingly she was waking up in the morning feeling as though she had stepped on board a train that had then suddenly picked up speed to such an extent that she was beginning to feel that it was running away with her.

So why had she allowed it to happen in the first place? After all no one had forced her.

No? When your king appealed to you personally for your help to save the future of your country, a country you loved, you didn't just turn round and say no, did you? At least not if you were a Carini.

The trouble was that, since she had said yes, the list of reasons why in her own interests she would have been better off saying no had begun to grow by the day.

'Via Venetii,' the *vaporetto* driver pointed out to her, interrupting her thoughts. 'The hotel, she is not far now. Is a very beautiful hotel. You go there before?'

'Yes,' Natalia told him. She could see from the expression on his face that the answer had sounded more curt than she had intended. But how could she explain to him how she felt about the fact that she had been obliged to sell her beloved spa hotel on Niroli to this one in Venice?

True, the choice of whom she should sell to had been her own. True, too, that she knew that the new owners, Maya and Howard, would uphold her own high standards, now that they had officially added her spa to their portfolio, but that still did not mean that she was not allowed to grieve for her much cherished and loved 'baby', did it?

So why give it up in the first place? Why give up the life she had worked so hard to build for herself to enter into an arranged marriage of state? So that she could be a princess? Natalia almost laughed out loud, the white flash of her even white teeth contrasting with the full warmth of her soft red lips making the driver of the *vaporetto* sigh in a way that caused Natalia to look away to conceal her amusement.

At twenty-nine she had had ample time to get used to her effect on the opposite sex.

To get used to her effect on the opposite sex, but never to fall in love. And now with her forthcoming marriage to the newly discovered heir to the Nirolian throne she was giving up the chance to do so for ever, wasn't she? After all, she wasn't foolish enough to think that a marriage arranged between two strangers by a king whose only thought was to secure the future of his kingdom could by some miracle turn into a passionately intense and lifelong love affair, was she? Not when she had never, ever fallen in love; not when her sole reason for agreeing to this marriage had been her passionate love, not for a man, but for a country, *her* country, just as her husband-to-be's desire was directed towards the throne of Niroli and not towards her. Could it work? Was she as mad as she was beginning to think to have agreed to marry Prince Kadir just so that she would be there at his side to ensure that he ruled her beloved country with wisdom and love? If only there were someone she could turn to for advice, but there wasn't. The king had forbidden her to discuss the matter with anyone.

The elegant and exclusive spa hotel that was her destination had its own landing stage. As she saw it approaching Natalia turned to pick up her bag. As she did so a man striding impatiently across the small square to the side of the hotel caught her eye, as much for any other reason as for his height. At almost six feet herself, she was appreciative of the visual impact of men who were taller than her, and this man was certainly that, taller, and broad shouldered, with surprisingly hard-packed muscles, too, for a man who looked as though he was closer to forty than thirty. Thick dark hair that just brushed the collar of his jacket gleamed with good health under the brilliant sunlight. His skin was warmly olive and although he was too far away for Natalia to see the colour of his eyes she could see the hard, precision hewn perfection of his facial bone structure with its high cheekbones and strong jaw. Here was a man, she acknowledged.

As though by some alchemic means he had somehow sensed her interest and paused, turning his head to look directly at her. She still could not see the colour of his eyes, but she could see that he was even more stunningly handsome face on than he had been in profile. It had to be the sun that was making her feel slightly dizzy and not the fact that he was looking at her... Had been looking at her, she recognised to her relief as he turned away and resumed his progress across the square. As the *vaporetto* pulled into the landing stage she admitted to herself that her brief interest in this man was not the wisest of things in a woman soon to enter into a dynastic marriage. How was she going to go on in that marriage if she was experiencing sexual desire for another man now? Sexual desire? That was ridiculous. She had simply been looking at him, that was all, and anyway he had gone now, and she was hardly likely to ever see him again, was she?

When Natalia arrived in the lobby, Maya hurried forward to hug her exuberantly. 'This is so good of you to come and help us with the transition of ownership. We wanted it to go smoothly and there's still so much to learn about your Nirolian spa. We had not dared to hope that you would be generous enough to come back to Venice so quickly.'

Natalia returned the hug a bit guiltily. It was impossible of course for her to tell her that the main reason she was back in Venice was because King Giorgio had wanted her out of the way until the newly discovered heir to the throne of Niroli had arrived on the island. Then she would be allowed to return and they would be presented, with full pomp and dignity, to the people of Niroli, along with the announcement of their marriage.

'But why can't I remain here?' she had questioned the king. 'After all I shall have to make arrangements for the future of the business.'

'You are a woman and I cannot permit you to remain

where you could be tempted to break the vow of secrecy I have sworn you to.'

She had of course been tempted to object to the use of that contemptuous 'you are a woman' but, knowing King Giorgio as she did, she had decided that there wasn't very much point, and then she had received the frantic plea to return to Venice to discuss the handover of the business with Maya and Howard. They had expressed their wish to buy some of her special formulae for the oils she used.

The truth was that, much as his old-fashioned attitudes often infuriated her, on this occasion, and perhaps against her own best interests, she had actually felt slightly sorry for the king when he had approached her with his unexpected proposition. He had run through each and every one of his potential male heirs in turn and been forced to reject them. Loving Niroli every bit as much as he did, she had fully understood his contrasting feelings of joy at the discovery that he had fathered an illegitimate son during a brief affair over forty years ago with an Arabian princess, and anxiety about offering this son the throne in case his son's Arabian upbringing meant that his ideas on how to rule were not suited to Niroli. And, yes, if she was honest it had been flattering—very flattering—to be told by King Giorgio that he had picked her out of all his single female subjects to become the wife of Niroli's future King because he had seen in her certain strengths and virtues that reminded him of his beloved first wife, Queen Sophia.

Everyone knew how much the people of Niroli had

loved and revered King Georigo's first wife and how much she had done for Niroli. As a little girl Natalia had woven foolish daydreams as children did of somehow going back in time to meet Queen Sophia and 'helping' her with her work. Now she had been given that opportunity in reality, or at least an opportunity to continue the work Queen Sophia had begun. At the time, filled with euphoria at the thought of her coming role in the future of her country, she hadn't thought marriage to a stranger too much of a price to pay. After all she had never been in love and had no expectation of being in love; she liked to think of herself as practically minded and she had embraced the idea of taking a marriage between two people with a common goal and making it work. Of course, even then she had had some doubts and concerns. Marriage to a future king meant producing that future king's heirs and spares, and that of course meant having sex with him. But King Giorgio had been too thrilled not to mention the fact that his secret son looked very like him, and since the king, even now in his old age, was a very good-looking man Natalia was assuming that her future husband was reasonably physically attractive.

What about his personality, though? she wondered and worried now. What if he was the kind of man she just could not grow to like or respect? If he was, she wouldn't want to abandon her country to him, would she? No, she would want to do what she could to offset those faults in him as his wife. Those who thought they knew her as a forward-thinking, successful businesswoman would, of course, be stunned and disbelieving when the news did break, and would no doubt question why she had not immediately refused to have anything whatsoever to do with the king's grand plan.

But then that was the trouble, wasn't it? Whilst on the surface she might appear to be all modern, she herself was something of an anomaly in that deep down inside her there was something else. That 'something' was her passionate and deep-rooted love for her country, for its past and its present but most of all for its future. Or rather the future it could have in the right hands. Because Niroli, like so much of the rest of the world, was at a crisis point where traditional values were clashing badly with modernity; where those on and off the island like herself, who wanted to see Niroli move forward into a future that guarded and protected its unique geographical benefits rather than wasted and abused them, were often in conflict with those who could see no reason not to squander Niroli's natural assets, or even worse those who sought to strip the island of its unique heritage in the name of progress by turning it into one huge tourist attraction.

What Natalia favoured was a different way, an eco-logically and Nirolian friendly way that would preserve the best of their traditions as well as move them forward into a prosperous future. She had never made any secret of her feelings about this. Her commitment to her other work, as an apothecary using natural oils and holistic treatments in the spa she had set up, was well known. However, as Natalia Carini she could only do so much and her sphere of influence was limited to those who for the most part shared her views. As Niroli's Queen she would be in a far, far more influential position to make very real and worthwhile changes. Certainly far more so than she did as the granddaughter of the island's acknowledged expert vintner.

'I'd be very happy to give you exclusive rights to some of my special oil recipes,' she told Maya now, switching her thoughts.

'We have been using the samples you were kind enough to give us during the negotiations for the purchase of your spa,' the sweet round faced Italian said, 'and our clients have raved about them. The deep muscle replenisher you have created for sportsmen has found particular favour and we have a growing client list of sportsmen already using our spas—skiers, football and polo players mainly—who come to us by word-of-mouth recommendation, and Howard has been panicking that we would soon run out of your oil.'

Natalia laughed. She was as responsive to flattery when it was genuine and given for the right reasons as anyone else, and it always delighted her when people reported favourably on her therapeutic oils.

'Then it is just as well perhaps that I took Howard's hint when he phoned last week and brought you a fresh supply with me,' she told Maya. Whilst she knew she could hardly continue to run a business once she was married to Prince Kadir, one thing Natalia did intend to stick out for was her own private space where she could continue to use her 'nose' as a perfumier—not to create new perfumes so much as to use the ingredients that went into them in a more therapeutic way. Just as music and now colour were both recognised as having healing properties, increasingly people were beginning to accept that scents also possessed the power to heal the body, the mind and the heart when blended and used properly. It was one of her dreams to create a range of scents that would do this, and now she had added to that a new dream of using her position as Niroli's Queen to set up a charity to distribute them to those in need.

'You will dine with us later this evening, I hope, but for now we thought you might welcome some free time to enjoy Venice, before we sit down together to talk over the mechanics of the purchase of your oil recipes.'

'That would suit me perfectly,' Natalia confirmed.

She laughed when Maya hugged her again and said emotionally, 'Oh, Natalia, I am so glad that you are willing to do this for us.'

As she returned Maya's grateful hug, Natalia acknowledged that she had been hoping to have a bit of time for herself, because there was one place in particular that she really wanted to go.

The late afternoon autumn mist stealing from the canals and swirling round the squares and streets created an atmosphere within the city that for her, whilst concealing it in the material sense, revealed it very sharply in an emotional sense. With the mist came a sombreness and a melancholy that she felt somehow truly reflected the deep hidden heart of the city, stripping from it the carnival mask it wore so easily for those it did not want to know its secrets. Natalia, though, had been coming here for many years, drawn back to it time after time, and there was no hesitation in her long-legged stride as

she made her way to the *vaporetto* stop from which the
water taxi would take her to the small glass-making
factory she had discovered years ago on her first visit
here. She had been awed and entranced then by the
beauty of the perfume bottles she had watched being
blown, and on each return trip she had revisited it,
choosing for herself a bottle that reflected in its unique
colours something of her mood of that visit. What would
catch her eye on this visit? she wondered. It was part of
the game not to anticipate what she would choose, but
simply to let it happen.

As she crossed the square she had seen earlier she
realised that she was following in the footsteps of the
man she had watched from the water taxi. Now what had
brought him into her thoughts? Not some ridiculous
idea that she might see him again? After the dismissive
look he had given her? When she was almost on the eve
of getting married? Fantasizing about tall, handsome
men glimpsed in the street hadn't been a folly she had
indulged in even when she was a teenager. Why was she
doing it now?

That was Venice for you, Natalia told herself ruefully.
It played tricks on the imagination and the eye, and in
more ways than one.

'Signorina, it is you. Ah, you grow more lovely with
every visit.'

Old Mario, the head of the family, gave her a gummy
smile as he welcomed her.

'And you grow more silver-tongued, Mario.' She
laughed, already looking past him towards the inner

sanctum where they kept their special one-off creations, like a small child anticipating Christmas, and salivating almost at the prospect of being allowed to choose just what she wanted.

Mario was turning away from her and she made to follow him, but his son stopped her.

'Please, we have something special for you this time. My father has made it himself. He said that he had this thought of you and that he felt he must do this thing…'

Natalia tried not to look as disappointed as she was feeling. She was strong-minded and independent enough to want to choose her own perfume bottle, but sensitively she didn't want to offend the old man.

He had disappeared into the back room and it seemed an age before he returned, carrying a battered cardboard box from which she could see tissue paper sticking out.

'Here,' he told her, proffering her the box.

Forcing a wide smile, Natalia took it, carefully unwrapping the tissue paper until she had revealed the small perfume bottle that lay within it. At first all she could see was every colour of the rainbow spliced with silver and gold and every nuance of beautiful colour and shade the human eye could imagine. It defeated her ability to rationalise what colour it actually was.

'Hold it in your hand,' the old man urged her.

A little hesitantly Natalia removed the bottle, and held it.

'Now look,' the shop owner commanded.

Natalia gasped as she stared at the bottle. It seemed to shimmer and glow as though it were still molten and not solid; as though it had a life force of its own that pulsated within it and, absurdly, she felt afraid to touch it, in case she harmed it.

'What...what is it?' she asked in an awed whisper.

'It is diamond glass, a very special and old recipe—we don't use it any more because it is not easily possible to come by the ingredients, and they have to be ground down and heated in such a way that makes it dangerous to the creator and the creation. Legend has it that only the Doge was allowed to own glassware made from this recipe, which was stolen from one of the great Caliphs of the East,' the younger boy explained wryly to her.

'It's so beautiful...'

'It is unique—possibly the last of its kind ever to be made and my father has made it for you. It is said that when the pure of heart hold the bottle it glows as it did just then for you, but when those who are motivated by darkness and evil touch the glass it grows dull and cold so that its colour vanishes.' He laughed. 'As yet we have not been able to confirm whether or not that is true, although my father swears that it is.'

The older man said something huskily in Venetian, which his son translated for Natalia even though she was able to do so herself.

'My father says that whenever you touch this bottle you will be reminded of the purity of your heart and the true beauty that comes from within. May it lift your spirits and warm your heart throughout your life.'

Tears filled Natalia's eyes. Increasingly she was beginning to worry that she might need raw warmth from outside her marriage to sustain her through it, and yet again she questioned whether she had made the right decision.

It was later than she had planned when Natalia finally left the factory and as she glanced at her watch she recognised that she was only just going to make it back to the spa hotel in time to join Maya and Howard for the pre-dinner drink they had offered her.

However, the minute she stepped into their private suite she realised that they had more to worry about than her being late for drinks. Maya was seated on one of the large room's three plain cream leather sofas, her right hand heavily bandaged and her arm in a sling.

'She slipped and dropped a glass bowl and then cut her hand on it,' Howard explained.

'And now we are in the most dreadful fix.' Maya sighed miserably. 'We had a phone call earlier, before I fell, from an unexpected client who is in between flights and who wanted to book in for the night. He plays polo and has an old injury that occasionally flares up. He requested the massage you showed me, Natalia, you know the one? The deep muscle massage you devised for sports injuries?'

Natalia nodded her head. The massage in question was one of her spa's specialities.

'When he was here last month I recommended it to him,' Maya continued, 'and he said it was most beneficial. Apparently these days he spends more time behind a desk than he does on the polo field and so this old injury occasionally flares up. Naturally I took the booking, and now he is expecting his massage in half an hour's time. He has taken our best suite, so he is not

someone we would want to offend. Now I can't do the
massage, and Gina, the only other masseuse we have
who could do it, is on holiday. I can't tell you how cross
with myself I am for doing something so stupid as
dropping that wretched bowl.'

Natalia sympathised with her. She could tell that
Maya was like her in that she set herself very exacting
standards and she knew just how she would be feeling
in her shoes. 'Couldn't I do the massage for you?' she
offered impulsively.

'Would you?' Immediately Maya was all relieved
and grateful smiles. 'We *were* hoping you might offer,'
she admitted honestly, adding, only half jokingly,
'Natalia, are you sure you would not like a partnership
with us? Only you would be the most wonderful asset
to the business.'

Don't tempt me, was Natalia's immediate private
reaction as she smiled and shook her head. The explanation she had given the other couple for her decision
to sell the spa had been her wish to focus on develop-
ing her skills as a perfumier. Another lie, but a necessary one, according to King Giorgio.

'What time is he booked in for?' she asked Maya
quietly, slipping into her professional persona.

'Half past. You've got twenty minutes to get ready.
I've already brought up a uniform for you. His name is
Leon Perez. Since his injury is a polo injury I imagine
he must be South American. He's requested the massage
in his suite, by the way, but there's nothing untoward in
that, as you will know. We do offer that facility.
However, if for any reason his behaviour *should* become

unacceptable, just press the buzzer at the side of the bed. We've had them installed in all of the rooms just in case. We intend to keep a list of those guests who mistake our services for those of a very different kind, so that we can make sure they don't repeat their mistake.'

'A wise precaution,' Natalia agreed. 'I did the same thing, although fortunately they haven't been used as yet.'

'When you've finished, we'll have drinks and dinner and continue our business discussions then,' Maya said as she handed Natalia a spa uniform.

The spa's uniform was a simple cap-sleeved, high-necked, linen-mix, A-line shift dress in plain white. The fabric was thick and heavy enough not to reveal what its wearer might be wearing underneath, Natalia noted approvingly. She liked the fact that Maya respected her employees enough not to give them a uniform that was in any way provocative. There was just about enough time for her to go to her own suite to shower, plait her hair to keep it out of the way and change into the uniform. It was rather shorter perhaps than she would have liked, and a bit tighter, but that was a problem one became accustomed to when one was tall and had a vo-luptuously curved hourglass figure. She gathered together everything Maya had given her that she would need before making her way to the guest's suite.

Natalia had given clients massages a hundred thousand times and more so there was no reason at all for that funny little sensation to curl its way through her stomach as she pressed the bell and then stood outside the suite waiting to be let in.

The suite door was being opened. A man was standing just inside it, wearing the ubiquitous white hotel bathrobe.

As she looked at him Natalia found that she was blinking dizzily in much the same way she had done when she'd first looked at the perfume bottle. It was *him*. Leon Perez was the man she had seen earlier, crossing the square. That it should be him was surely against all the laws of reason and logic, and yet there was no mistake. It was him. Her senses were telling her that very loudly and clearly. Her *senses*. What right had they to get themselves involved in what was after all a purely professional matter? This was dreadful. And what was worse, far worse, was that everything she had just told herself about there being no need for her to feel anxious had just been blown totally out of the water by the force of one single look from those impossibly long-lashed jade green eyes.

Her heart swung crazily through her chest as though suspended from a pendulum and then stopped dead. She felt as though she were drowning in the depths of his eyes; as though she were being sucked under by some powerful sensual undertow come out of nowhere to possess her. Through the clamouring tumult of her senses she could think only one clear thought. And that was how very, very badly she wanted him.

CHAPTER TWO

WHAT *was* this…this lightning dart of pure volcanic sexual desire shooting up inside Natalia to spill past the long-closed gates of her own restraint, melting them into nothing?

Leave! Leave now, an inner voice was urging her. You can't afford this. Just turn around and go…because if you don't…

'You booked a massage?'

Too late…too late. *Why* hadn't she done what that inner voice had urged her? she wondered shakily as she stepped into the warm womb of semi darkness that was the dimly lit foyer of the suite. Her 'nose', so sensitive always, too much sometimes, went into overdrive. She was being overwhelmed by the flood of scents washing over her, the new decorations smell of paint and carpet and fibres all mingled together. The scent of the lilies in the hallway, overlaying the special signature perfume she had created for herself and always wore, a special recipe based on roses, with a hint of musk sharpened with the unique oil she had produced by blending grapes as they ripened, and vines as they thrust out new growth, maturity blended with the raw, powerful surge of new life. Normally it pleased and soothed her, but now was distorted perhaps by the smell of her own fear and she discovered that she was fighting against its unfamiliar demanding sensuality.

But most powerful of all was the scent of *him*. Images flashed inside her head; heat; the scent of something alien and unknown to her carried on a hot wind, the scent of male power both physical and mental; a rawness and vitality merging into something so intimate that she felt almost as though he had physically imprisoned her. Something dangerous and very unwanted was happening to her, Natalia admitted, grand slamming her senses, rushing over her and through her, forcing her to surrender to it.

'This way.'

With a tremendous effort Natalia forced herself to ignore what she was feeling. For a moment she had wanted him. So what? That was probably just a knee-jerk reaction to her own knowledge that her unplanned years of celibacy were shortly to be brought to an end via her marriage. There was perhaps nothing like recognising that something was about to be taken 'off the menu' for it suddenly to be extraordinarily desirable. As for that dizzy, soft-boned feeling sliding through her like warmed precious oils, *that* was probably caused by the unfamiliar act of having to tilt her head back to look up at him, instead of him being on her own eye level as most men were. How tall was he, exactly?

King Giorgio had not offered her any information as

to the physical make-up of his illegitimate son, other than his very proud boast that he was 'obviously his son'. All she knew about him was that he was forty years old, had never been married, and had been brought up as a sheikh-in-waiting, but that on being offered the throne of Niroli he had handed over the rulership of Hadiya to his younger half brother.

There had been days since she had agreed to the king's proposition when it had been a hard call *not* picturing someone squat, plump and wearing too much gold, especially in his teeth, despite King Giorgio's obvious admiration for him.

In contrast, this man was six feet three at least, powerfully muscled without an ounce of excess weight and, as for his teeth, well, that small chip in one of the front pair suggested that despite their excellent shape and colour they were all his own. It would be wonderful to dance with a man whose height was so perfectly devised by nature to physically match her own. Just to dance, what about…? She tensed her body against what she was thinking. It was tilting her head that was responsible for her out-of-character response to him, she told herself feverishly. After all, at that angle the flow of blood to the brain would be diminished and that alone would be enough to induce…to induce what? Mind blowing images of such sensory sensuality that her nerve endings felt stripped of their protective covering.

For such a tall and powerfully built man he moved very lightly and easily—and very confidently, walking ahead of her, leaving her to follow in his wake like some harem woman following her master? Now where on earth had that idea come from? This man was South American, Maya had told her.

Maya and Howard had chosen to renovate the interior of the small palazzo they had transformed into their spa hotel in a way that was naturally holistic and an example of pared-down minimalism. The luxurious comfort of its rooms and décor came from the quality of the natural furnishings and fabrics they had used. This suite, the most exclusive of all the rooms, had plain off-white walls to offset its marble floors. All the rooms had specially designed massage tables in addition to their huge king-sized beds.

'You booked one of the spa's special neck and back massages,' Natalia checked as they approached the massage table.

'Yes. And let me warn you, you had better know what you are doing.'

He sounded almost antagonistic towards her, something that Natalia wasn't used to either as a woman or as a professional, and somehow, instead of dampening down the unwanted feverish intensity of her reaction to him, it only seemed to inflame it. Was she really so immature? Wanting what she couldn't have because she couldn't have it? That was ridiculous. She just wasn't that kind of person.

Perhaps now wasn't the time to tell him that she was the one responsible for creating the massage in the first place, Natalia admitted, even if his attitude towards her had put her on her mettle. She knew without vanity that she was an excellent masseuse—it was a gift and an instinct she had known she possessed virtually from childhood, this power to soothe and heal with the touch of her hands. Had she been doing this in her own spa she would have been talking with her clients, drawing them out about themselves whilst she assessed which of her own specially blended oils would suit their needs best. She had no intention of trying that with this man though. She had no idea why she should feel this instinctive awareness of a need to protect herself from him.

Don't you? an inner voice taunted her. Take a good look at him—that should tell you. No woman with red blood in her veins could fail to be affected by his maleness, especially not one who has just agreed to a passionless dynastic marriage.

Was that it? Was her unexpected and definitely unwanted reaction to him solely some unfamiliar last-minute and reckless desire to rebel against her own decision; a reminder by her senses of just what she would be giving up? She had never been promiscuous, she reminded herself, so why on earth should her senses suddenly have her physically yearning for an unknown man now? Physically yearning? She was doing no such thing! Yes, you are, her senses responded smartly. Determinedly Natalia fought to subdue them. She was here to work, nothing else. Just to work.

He had his back to her now and was stripping off the spa's robe, letting it drop to the floor. Natalia held her breath. If he was nude, beneath the robe—and he certainly had the kind of male confidence that would mean that he could quite easily be. But he wasn't. And she wasn't prepared to let herself know whether she was pleased or disappointed to see that he had a small towel wrapped around his hips. Far better from a masseur's point of view than underwear, it showed her that he was familiar with this kind of experience. How many other foolish women had felt as she was feeling right now? Had he looked at them as indifferently as he was looking at her or had they seen desire for them in those dark green eyes? From out of nowhere like a fierce tornado, jealousy gripped hold of her. The shock of it made her hands tremble as she waited for him to lie face down on the table.

She was, Natalia discovered, holding in her breath, and no wonder, when she saw the way those superbly defined muscles rippled with pure male strength. Yes, he was obviously a horseman, she acknowledged—those thighs certainly indicated that. And as for him being a polo player—he certainly had the requisite muscle structure, and the wealth if the understated but still discreetly logoed expensive watch and the fact that he was in this suite were anything to go by. His flesh shone a subtle warm bronze in the room's lights, moving sleekly over the heavy padding of his muscles. He moved like a hunting cheetah, light on his feet, swift, silent and deadly. If she had not known he was South American she suspected that she might have put him down as Italian, although there was something within the devastatingly hard-boned masculinity of his face that hinted at a cultural legacy she could not quite define, something alien—and challenging to her as a woman? Ignore it, she warned herself speedily, trying to focus on other aspects of her client. His manner was certainly European, and yet it was also not. Because he was South American? Irritatingly that something 'other' for some reason was nagging at her subconscious, trying to tell her something, though she didn't know what. More out of habit than anything she turned away whilst he settled himself on the massage table.

An important part of this particular form of massage was the mood music and lighting that accompanied it. Maya had instructed her how to activate the sound and light systems, both pretty similar to her own, although she preferred whenever possible to open the windows and have the simple sounds of nature as the only auditory accompaniment to her massage. But then of course she also used her oils and she was a great believer in not overloading the senses with too many strong stimuli at once.

She poured a small amount of oil into the waiting bowl and warmed it over a tea light and then poured a very small amount into her own cupped palm.

'This massage is designed to work on tensions and blocks within the deep muscle structure,' she explained calmly. 'You may find that it gives rise to the occasional uncontrollable movement of one or other of those muscles depending on the degree of stress they are under, but that's completely normal.'

The sound of him exhaling conveyed his impatience far more effectively than any words could have done—and his desire for her to keep her distance from him by not talking. Well, that certainly suited her.

She started to sweep her hands over his skin, assessing the tone and texture of the muscles beneath it, breathing evenly and slowly as she let herself sink down into and be absorbed into her gift for her work. So many things could be learned by this silent communication of touch and flesh, so many secrets withdrawn—he, for instance, was tensing himself against her even though he might be pretending with his steady, even breathing not to be doing so. At some stage in his life he had fallen heavily on his left hip, possibly from a horse. Polo again? There was no obvious damage but she could feel the muscle's sensitive flutter as it whispered to her of its secret trauma. Automatically she responded to its need, stroking first reassurance and then, once it had accepted her touch, using a deeper, more searching kneading technique to send strength back into it, giving it power and confidence, telling it with her touch that it need not fear, that it could trust itself.

His hair, thick and dark—darker than her own, in fact—would, as she already knew, brush his collar when he was dressed. Now it felt sweetly soft against her fingertips as she swept up over his back and searched out the tensions in his neck muscles. She had been working for nearly fifteen minutes and her own muscles were beginning to ache slightly. Beneath the A-line shift all she was wearing was a pair of boy shorts, a practical decision, she had thought, but one she was regretting now as the movements required by the massage had brought her nipples into the kind of contact with the shift dress that was making them swell and ache. At least she assumed it was the fabric of her uniform.

She had never seen, never mind touched, a man with such a perfect body. She wanted to go on stroking and learning his flesh for ever. The feel of it intoxicated and delighted her whilst the scent of his massage-warmed skin was surely the scent of sensuality and sex itself, distilled to perfection. It possessed her 'nose' as physically and completely as though he had actually taken possession of her, causing a weakening of her own muscles and a corresponding ache deep within her belly, a sense of mingling heat and need that flowed up through her, affecting her like alcohol might do a drinker, melting bonds of her inhibitions and taking from her her ability to make rational decisions or to think rational thoughts. Her fingertips traced the long length of his spine, delicately tracing each vertebra. No wonder he stood so tall and proud. She had reached the edge of the towel wrapped low on his hips now. Since his request had been for a deep-textured neck and upper back massage there was no reason for her to be touching his body here. No reason other than her own need to indulge herself. All bodies had their strengths and their weaknesses, their good and their bad, but this body, his body, was so perfectly constructed that the pleasure of touching it was acting on her like a drug. Automatically her fingertips eased down the towel and sought the small indents either side of his spine just above the covered curve of his buttocks. She breathed in slowly and closed her eyes, stroking and circling, savouring the rush of pleasure surging through her as she caressed him.

'What the hell...?'

The angry curse with which he rejected her unplanned intimacy made her step back, exhaling shakily as her face started to burn at her own lack of professionalism, and then stand completely still as though transfixed. When he had moved away from her he had started to turn over. As he had done so the towel had slipped from his body allowing her to see that, no matter what that angry curse might have been intended to convey, the real evidence of the effect of her touch on him was there for her to see in the thick, strong erection he had inadvertently revealed.

Natalia couldn't take her gaze off it. He wasn't the first client with a hard-on she had ever seen, of course; it was a natural and automatic male reaction to female touch, after all, she reminded herself. But this was the first time she had reacted like this to a client. Massage was a form of therapy and healing; she did not use it as an aid to turning herself on. By rights she should apologise, but what was there for her to say? That she had loved the feel of his flesh so much she had wanted to have more of it? Hardly. She bent down, intending to pick up his robe and hand it to him. Out of the corner of her eye she could see that he was getting up off the massage table. Would he complain about her to Maya and Howard?

How embarrassing would that be, given the true nature of her business relationship with them? She held out the robe to him, determined not to look at him, but some power greater than her own was obviously at work because against all logic she was reaching out and running her fingertip down the dark line of hair that would take her in only one direction.

She felt him contract his stomach muscles. Against her touch or against his reaction to it?

'Look,' she heard him saying bitingly, 'I don't

want…' And then abruptly he stopped speaking and swung his legs to the floor, reaching for her as he did so.

The shock of feeling his hands on her flesh beneath her shift sliding up her bare thighs, and then further until his fingers were massaging the rounded curves of her buttocks beneath her underwear, jolted through her, making her shudder in violent mindless pleasure. She could smell as well as feel her own arousal, with its familiar sleek wetness and softly swollen flesh. She had thought she had gone beyond the hyper-sexuality of those late teenage years when learning about her body and its reactions, along with learning about her own desires, had been safely in a haven of deliberately chosen abstinence, where not experiencing sexual desire had been something she had accepted and preferred. But now she was having the security of that comfort wrenched from her, leaving her naked and exposed to what she was feeling. And as to what she was feeling…

Natalia was fighting hard to suppress her unwanted and unacceptable desire, but already she could feel the gathering tightness presaging an orgasm. As though a switch had been thrown inside that part of her mind that regulated how she thought and felt, suddenly she wasn't sensible, respectable Natalia Carini, bride-to-be of Prince Kadir, but a far more pagan Natalia, who was all hedonistic, sensual woman. Instinctively she struggled to hold back her body's response—not now out of rejection of her orgasm, but instead because, shockingly, this other Natalia actively wanted to prolong each millisecond of pleasure for as long as she could. Everything about Leon Perez dominated her senses, in a way that flooded past her defences. She had nothing within her experience to hold up to herself as a pattern card of what she could do to stop what she was feeling, because quite simply she had never, ever felt like this before. She longed, not just to touch him, but to taste him as well, to hear the sound of his breathing in the last seconds before he lost control, ragged and tortured in his need to possess her. She wanted to smell the hot, aroused male scent of him as it mingled with her own scent, creating a new fragrance that was unique to them, as potent and alive in its own way as though between them they had created a new life.

But most of all she wanted the experience of feeling him within her, her flesh sheathing his and holding it, her muscles stroking the most pleasurable of all pleasures into his, drawing the essence of life itself from him as sweetly and perfectly as she knew how to draw the essence of its perfume from a flower. It bemused her that she, who prided herself on her mature restraint, should not only feel this depth of passion, but actively relish giving in to it. Why? Because she was about to get married? Because she had not had sex in such a long, long time? Because of him, the man himself?

Of the three options the one she preferred was the second, but wilfully her brain refused to accept her offer of it. The warning of the closed door brought about by her marriage, then? It had to be that. It could not be him, this man. It must not be, she told herself determinedly, knowing she could not allow herself to accept what that might mean.

'Who are you? What are you…?' she could hear him

demanding thickly as he slid the shift from her body. 'Or need I ask? No, don't tell me,' he answered his own question. 'Because we both know the answer. You are what your sex knows so well how to be, deceit, full of promises and tricks, all things to all men, for so long as it pleases you to be.' There was a hard contempt in his voice matched with bitterness and anger, but Natalia was oblivious to its warning and had no sensual space left to hear it, anyway. She was totally lost in the dark surf like curl of pleasure she was riding. Her soft, husky purr of approval at their intimacy swelled into the soft notes of the music and became part of it. Never once had her thoughts ever even come close to conjuring up a fulfilment for her as all consuming as the one her senses told her she would have with this magnificent male. It felt so right to want him as completely as she did. They were standing body to body, the aching pressure between her legs growing with every breath she took. She leaned forward, breathing in the scent of his flesh, and then, placing her lips against it, she stroked her hands down over him.

'No!'

The harshness of his rejection shocked through her. Her heart was thudding in uneven beats.

'You may have stolen from the other men you have shared your body with their right to be in control of your pleasure, but you will not do so with me,' he warned her. 'Where I come from it is the man who leads and the woman who follows, not the other way around. It is the man who takes and the woman who gives.' His hands were on her body, stroking far too slowly upwards towards her breasts, causing her breathing to become an uneven, jagged sound of repressed need.

Her breasts had become so engorged with arousal that the ache of her tightly stretched nipples had almost become a physical pain. When he touched one, cupping her breast and rubbing the pad of his thumb-tip over it, she cried out in raw need.

'Your flesh is the colour of almond milk brushed with sunset and gold. It demands the homage of a man's touch and it seeks to enslave him. But I will not be enslaved.'

Natalia could barely focus on his poetic words. She was on fire with the intensity of her own aching need. She reached up and placed her hands either side of his face, drawing him down towards her body, driven by her longing to feel his mouth against her flesh, and already ready to cry out with disappointment when he refused her.

And then to her disbelief he did something she had never in her wildest dreams imagined any man doing. He picked her up bodily in his arms and carried her over to the bed. She was just under six feet, and, whilst narrow-waisted, she was voluptuously curved and yet he was carrying her as though she were a size 00 and skin and bones. It was ridiculous to feel so thrilled and awed by such a basic display of masculinity, but yet she still was.

'Now,' he told her as he placed her on the bed and leaned over her. 'Now I shall take from you what you are so willing to give me, even though my intellect tells me that it is a worthless offering worn thin by the hands of all the others who have possessed you before me.'

He was insulting her, but she was too aroused to check him and to retaliate that of the two of them she suspected his tally of past intimate partners would be far greater than hers. He was an adult male, after all, nearing forty, she suspected. A very sexual adult male, whereas she was a woman who had been celibate for what she now knew to be dangerously too long. Instead she arched up in obedience to the touch of the male hands shaping her, learning her, and then whilst she cried out and moved urgently against him he knew her with their touch, stroking open the secret places of her sex with the art a skilled perfumier might bring to drawing the most precious essence from deep within the heart of a rose. Somehow it was as though by his touch he were in some elemental way taking her apart and rebuilding her to fit his own desire, a sensual alchemist using the dark power of his sexuality to transmute her flesh into his creature. And she knew she would not have had it any differently. Her senses revelled in every small nuance of her own arousal and response, the lips of her sex swelling and opening eagerly to give him the glistening sweetness of her pleasure. Through just the touch of his fingertip he drew from her the sweet agony with ecstasy she had tried to hold at bay, earlier.

'No,' he commanded thickly, 'don't close your eyes.'

Obediently she gave him the eye contact he was demanding, holding nothing back as she allowed him to look past her barriers and share with her all that she was experiencing. Never, ever had she known such a powerful sense of being possessed. It consumed her utterly, leaving only the shell of her previous sexual self.

Her gaze heavy with her retreating pleasure, she

watched as he parted her legs and positioned himself between them.

From somewhere he had produced the necessary means of protection, the rustle of its packaging striking a distant note of reassurance, even whilst a part of her still mourned the accompanying loss of the sensory pleasure of skin-to-skin, flesh-to-flesh intimacy with him.

From his first thrust within her Natalia knew what she had not wanted to let herself imagine; that this man was so perfectly physically formed for her that every particle of her responded to that knowledge. Her body opened softly and moistly for him, still sensitised by the pleasure he had already given it, holding him and gripping him, glorying in the width and the strength of him, tiny quivers of pre-orgasmic pleasure rippling through her as she lifted her hips and wrapped her toned body around him, wanting to draw him as deep within herself as she could. She could hear the thunder of their mutual heartbeat, shaking both their bodies; she could taste the warmth of his breath, smell the aroused heat of his flesh as it mingled with her own scent. With each thrust he took her deeper and higher, and with each counter movement she urged him on until there was no more climbing to be done, only that final leap together into eternity itself.

Natalia drew a shuddering breath of shocked disbelief. From the bathroom she could hear the sound of the shower running. She slid from the bed, pulling on her underwear and her shift with clumsy fingers. What had she done? No one must ever know about this. No one!

Her anger against herself clawed at the back of her throat. How could she have been so reckless and so foolish? And for what? To have sex with a stranger? How sleazy that sounded. How against everything she believed about her own respect for herself.

The shower was still running. She had to get out of here before he came back. She was dressed now and, with no reason to stay and any number not to do so, why was she delaying?

Go, go now, she urged herself, before he comes back and humiliates you even more. Even *more*? Could there be any deeper humiliation than those words he had said to her as the final surges of her pleasure had subsided.

'Right,' he had told her tersely, as he had withdrawn from her and got up off the bed. 'You've had what you wanted, now go.'

What *she* had wanted! He had wanted it—*her*—too, hadn't he? Of course he had. But she had initiated it, hadn't she? And that was certainly something she had never done before.

She opened the door into the corridor, relieved to see that it was empty, and then hurried towards the lift that would take her down to her own room on the floor below. Thank God Maya had said he was leaving first thing in the morning. What had happened between them was a secret she would keep to herself for the rest of her life. For her own sake and for Niroli's. And thank God, too, for that safety-ensuring rustle she could hear echoing inside her head. At least that meant that the only repercussions from her uncharacteristic behaviour would be her ones she would carry within her senses and her conscience in secret.

How could she not feel conscience-stricken? After all, she wasn't just feeling guilty and suffused with shame because her behaviour went against her own personal moral code. There was also her awareness of her additional responsibility to the role she was about to play and the fact that she was about to become the wife of Niroli's future King. How could she have been so lost to all sense of what was right and proper and responsible as to have transgressed against the code she knew her agreement to marry Prince Kadir automatically enforced on her? As a royal bride, a royal wife, it would be of paramount importance that she was seen to be beyond any kind of moral reproach. She knew that King Giorgio would more than likely have had discreet enquiries made into her sexual past and had no doubt been reassured by her long-standing period of celibacy.

She must not dwell on what had happened. She must put it right out of her mind now. Either that or she must go to King Giorgio and tell him that she could not marry Prince Kadir. The surge of emotion that gripped her appalled her. So what if she was free? That did not mean that he…this Leon Perez would want her again. No, what she was thinking was crazy. So crazy that it scared her. And besides, she had her duty to think of, her already-given commitment. No, her mind was made up, her future decided, and it would not be a future filled with the sickness of longing for a man who had already made it plain just how he felt about her.

Like someone fearing drowning, Natalia clung to the

knowledge that she was committed to marrying Prince Kadir. What she had done was dreadful, unforgivable, appalling—a form of madness. She must learn to accept and then forget it as some last-minute form of prenuptial panic that her senses had sprung on her. Something that was now over and done with and in the past, whilst she must look towards her already-planned future.

CHAPTER THREE

KADIR looked grimly round the now-empty bedroom. She had gone. Good. The music she had left playing was still on and the dimmed lights were far too evocative a reminder of what had happened, but nowhere near as compelling as the scent of her, which seemed to cling to his own flesh despite his shower. It was an unusual blend of sensual warmth spiced with something he couldn't name, and it had insinuated itself into his awareness in a way that infuriated him.

What was he doing wasting time thinking about her? She was nothing to him. Nothing, just a woman who was a sexual opportunist. He wouldn't have gone near her if it hadn't been for the fact that a near deathbed promise wrung from him by his dying mother that he end his relationship with his mistress had resulted in a period of celibacy far longer than he was used to. That was the only reason for what had happened, the only explanation there could be.

After all, it hardly suited the new roles he was about to take on, of both King-in-waiting and newly married man, for him to be having sex with a stranger; a masseuse, for heaven's sake. What had happened to his self-control? He normally found it easy to control his sexual appetite. She hadn't even been his type—he liked petite women, not sensual Amazons with lush curves and demanding sexual appetites. Yet he had allowed his loins to rule his head.

Well, it certainly must not happen again—not with any woman.

Kadir had no intention of being one of those rulers who pretended to have a certain moral stance in public whilst freely indulging in the most salacious of habits in private. There had never been a time in his life when sensual promiscuity had appealed to him. There had been women, yes, especially during his years on the professional polo circuit, but those were long behind him now and the only women to share his bed these last years had been a modest succession of discreet mistresses, of which Zahra had been the latest.

He had known her for many years, but they had only become lovers after her husband's death. From his point of view it had been a very convenient and practical arrangement. Kadir liked such arrangements; emotions weren't something he wanted to bring into his relationships, and an over-emotional mistress was the last thing he wanted. Or had been. Surely now the last thing he wanted was an emotional new wife.

It had been some financial business connected with his late mother's estate that had brought him to Venice, and he was glad now that he had without thinking booked into the hotel using his alias from his polo-playing days.

From what he had learned about King Giorgio his father might have enjoyed a pretty varied sex life himself, but he had very strict views on the conduct of current members of the Nirolian royal family, especially his own heir.

Kadir's frown deepened. Should she discover who he was and try to make use of that information, he might be forced to defend his behaviour to his father and the thought of that was totally unpalatable. How could he have put himself in such a situation? And with such a woman; the very antithesis of everything he personally wanted to see in a woman—especially one who shared his bed.

It was lucky that he had had the means of protection to hand, otherwise… Otherwise he would have stopped; there was no question of that. How could there be? He had a responsibility, after all, not just to himself, but to the woman he was committed to marrying. Was he really so sure that he could have stopped? Kadir swore inwardly as he ground the taunting inner voice into silence.

It was too late now to wish that he hadn't come to Venice. His mother had loved the city. 'It is like a miracle to those of us born of the desert to live in a city of water,' she had once told him.

Kadir's mouth hardened with bitterness. He had thought he had known his mother; had believed he shared a special closeness with her, but he had been deceiving himself just as she had deceived him. The last thing he had expected in those final days before she had finally succumbed to the fatal illness that had stalked her all summer was to hear her tell him that the man he had always thought of as his father had been no such thing and that, instead, he was the result of a youthful affair she had had with a European. And not just any European, but King Giorgio of Niroli, the head of what was reputed to be Europe's richest royal family. Not that money was of any primary concern to him. Kadir had turned the million-plus inheritance he had received from his maternal grandfather into a billion-figure empire before he had reached his thirtieth birthday, thanks to his own financial and entrepreneurial skills. No, he had no need of King Giorgio's wealth, and no real need either of the title he would inherit from him, but what he did need was to find out if this new persona his mother's revelations had given him fitted him more comfortably than the one he had always previously worn. And if didn't? If he felt as alien and apart from those he lived amongst as King Giorgio's son and heir as he had done as Hadiya's sheikh, then what? Then he would just have to live with it. He was forty now, after all, not an untried boy who knew nothing of himself. Niroli would give him the chance to stretch himself, to prove himself in many ways that ruling Hadiya could not. Besides, it was too late now for him to change his mind. He had given his commitment to his brother, Ahmed, to support his claim to become Hadiya's new sheikh and he had also given his commitment to his as yet unmet father to become Niroli's next King.

But whilst the outcome of his mother's revelations might ultimately be to his benefit, Kadir could not overcome his sense of betrayal that his mother could have kept something so important to him a secret.

She had begged him to understand and to forgive

her, telling him that she had already been promised in marriage to her husband when she had met King Giorgio. She'd stopped off on the island of Niroli on her way home to Hadiya. According to her, theirs had been an intensely passionate and equally intensely brief affair, and her marriage to her husband had taken place before she had realised she was carrying King Giorgio's child.

'So why tell me now,' he had demanded angrily, 'since you have not seen fit to do so before?'

'Before I was afraid for you,' she had told him. 'Everyone assumed that you were the legitimate heir to the sheikdom and I could not bear to be responsible for taking that from you. But now…I am close to death, my son, and I have watched you these last weeks since your uncle died. For all that you are ready to assume your responsibilities to Hadiya I can see that you do not have the heart to do so. You have always yearned to be free of the restrictions our small kingdom has imposed on you. Where your brother is content to go and count the revenues from Hadiya's oil wells and listen to the state advisers, you could never exist beneath the yoke of another's rule.

'There is something I want you to do for me, Kadir.'

That was when she had produced the small gold amulet, worn and thin and decorated with ancient writing.

'King Giorgio gave me this. I want you to return it to him for me—and in person. I have kept an interest in his world over the years and I understand that King Giorgio is in despair because he does not have a direct male heir to inherit the throne from him. You are his son, Kadir. Your rightful place is on the throne of Niroli, not here in Hadiya where I have always known you have never quite felt at home. Oh, you have tried, but I have seen your impatience with our ways, and your desire to live a different kind of life. You have learned the subtleties of the way we in the East do business, but I have seen in your eyes that you are impatient of it and that you yearn for the directness of your European heritage.'

'If by that you mean that I resent the paying of large bribes to already wealthy men when the poorest of our world go without, then, yes, I do grow impatient,' he had agreed tersely.

She had died three days after making her confession to him, and Kadir knew that his gentle brother had been shocked by his inability to shed any tears for her.

Women! What sane man would ever trust one? He had learned young about their duplicity. He had been just eighteen when he had discovered that the bride chosen for him by his family was far from being the innocent sweet virgin she was supposed to be and had in fact been having an affair with a married cousin for over a year. It wouldn't be true to say that the discovery of her deceit had broken his heart. He had broken off the betrothal—it had been an arranged marriage, after all—but it had certainly taught him to mistrust the female sex. They lied when it suited them to do so, with their kisses and their protestations of love, and far more importantly they lied about their fidelity. He had learned that much the hard way. What infuriated him now, though, was that, knowing what he did, he had still given way too easily to his own physical desire for the woman who had just left him. Why? Why? Because his need to possess her had been stronger than anything he had ever experienced. That was rubbish, he denied his inner voice angrily. Total rubbish. She had been the one who had come on to him, after all. And he had been the one who had taken her, so filled with need for her that he couldn't stop himself. A moment's aberration, that was all…a nothing…to be obliterated as though it had never been, like an empty Bedouin camp covered by the desert sands.

He looked down at the amulet he was holding. It had still been warm from her own flesh when his mother had handed it to him and sometimes when he held it in his hand and closed his eyes he could almost convince himself that he could still feel the echo of an imprint of that warmth on it. As a boy he had thought his mother the most beautiful and wonderful woman in the whole world, and she in turn had adored him. Adored him but kept from him the truth about his parentage.

When she had given him the amulet she might have had some romantic idea of him turning up on Niroli barefoot and ragged from some solitary and arduous odyssey spent journeying to claim his birthright and being welcomed by his father with tears of joy. But modern life wasn't like that.

Far from travelling like some would be Ulysses he had initially simply and discreetly let it be known through the right diplomatic channels that he and the King of Niroli needed to make personal contact with one another.

The result had been a flurry of letters and telephone calls interspersed with terse emails from the king's more

IT-savvy advisers, and a DNA test to establish the truth of his mother's claim, all without he and King Giorgio ever speaking personally to one another, never mind setting eyes on one another.

Cynically he was inclined to suspect that it was the result of the DNA test that had ultimately led to King Giorgio's formal offer to him of the throne of Niroli.

Further negotiations had followed once he had been able to establish that his brother was willing to step in and rule Hadiya in his place. Negotiations during which he had raised his own concerns about the willingness of the people of Niroli to accept him as their absolute ruler. King Giorgio's response to his concern had been to suggest that a diplomatic marriage should be arranged for him with a Nirolian woman who would be welcomed as their queen by the people.

Historically in Arab society there was no right of primogeniture—a man made his way within his extended family by his own skills and strengths and he married where he could achieve the best bargain for himself in terms of the benefits the marriage would bring. And therefore Kadir had no issues with the fact that his wife-to-be was the granddaughter of the island's most senior vintner. What she was bringing to the marriage bargain would be of far more value to him that any supposed blue blood.

With everything organised for him to fly direct from Hadiya to Niroli at the end of the week, this matter of his mother's still-outstanding Venetian bank account and business interests had needed resolving, and so he had flown here *en route,* reawakening an old polo injury ache in doing so, hence his decision to book into the spa, which he knew was one favoured by top sportsmen and women.

In the morning he was leaving by private jet for Niroli. The king had been quite specific that he did not want his people to know of their relationship until he himself presented him to them as his son and their new King-to-be, followed by an immediate announcement of his marriage to Natalia Carini, and, being the man he was, Kadir had thought that it made good sense to arrive ahead of schedule just to see how his father would react. From what he had heard of him King Giorgio was an autocratic ruler who refused to delegate, or allow his country to change.

Kadir intended to make it plain to him that if *he* was to rule then he fully intended to rule alone and on his own terms.

He looked at the door again. Where had she gone? To another man's bed? His fist closed round the amulet, and then he made a sound of angry self-disgust as he turned on his heel and picked up his laptop. He had more important things to do than think about a promiscuous pleasure-giver whom he would never see again—nor would ever want to see again.

As she walked across the square Natalia was oblivious to the admiring looks she was attracting from passersby. Yesterday's mist had turned into a soft drizzly rain that lay like diamond drops on the darkness of her hair, causing its soft waves to turn into rebellious curls. She wasn't doing this in the hope of seeing Leon Perez and she certainly hadn't humiliated herself by checking the register to see if he had actually checked out this morning. No, she was crossing the square because she needed some fresh air, some space inside her head in which to come to terms with her own horror at what she had done. The only saving grace of the whole incident, if it could be called such, was the fact that he Leon Perez thankfully—mercifully—had used protection, so she need have no concerns about there being any repercussions of any kind from their intimacy. It made her feel physically sick to think of the potential consequences if he hadn't done. How could she have been so lost to everything to have taken such a risk—to her own health, to the trust King Giorgio had placed in her, to her husband-to-be's right to expect her to come to him free of any kind of taint from another relationship?

She could see a coffee shop up ahead of her and she ducked into its crowded warmth. Her mobile started to ring. She put down her cappuccino so that she could answer the call.

'The king wishes you to return to Niroli immediately,' she heard the voice of the king's most senior minister informing her tersely.

'Immediately? But why?'

'I cannot tell you any more.'

'But my flight back is booked for the day after tomorrow, and I don't know if I can—'

'A private flight has been arranged for you. All you need to do is present yourself at the special check-in desk at the airport.'

'But why? What is going on?' Natalia started to demand but it was too late; the King's Chief Minister had already ended the call.

'Have you finished with the table?'

'What? Oh, yes,' she confirmed, getting up to let the two young women take over the table.

Outside it was still drizzling. Niroli had a warm and sunny climate all year round, rather like that of the Canaries, albeit with seasonal fluctuations, and the drizzle and its accompanying grey skies made her shiver.

What was behind the urgent summons of her to return ahead of schedule?

Had the new heir changed his mind about their marriage and, if so, how did she feel about that? Natalia wondered just over a couple of hours later when she had been escorted on board her private flight to Niroli.

'What would you like to drink?' the smiling steward was asking her. 'We have champagne?'

Natalia could feel the movement of the sleek modern jet as it started to roll down the runway. A feeling of panic gripped her but she swiftly controlled it. This was it, she was on her way—not just home, but to her future and her future husband. 'No…no champagne, thank you,' she told the steward hollowly. 'Just water, please.'

CHAPTER FOUR

'BUT this is ridiculous,' Natalia objected to the driver of the imposing chauffeur-driven car that had been waiting for her right on the runway the moment her plane touched down. 'I don't want to go to the palace; I want you to take me home.'

'I'm sorry, but my orders are to take you to the palace,' the driver told her woodenly.

Natalia stared out of the blacked-out windows in frustrated silence. This was crazy. What on earth was going on? Why on earth hadn't an official from the palace been waiting in the car for her to explain everything?

The sky had turned clear blue-green, and was now shading into midnight-blue velvet as darkness fell and the car sped along the modern ceremonial highway linking the palace and the main town to the airport.

Up ahead of them Natalia could see the lights of the town itself, crowned by the familiar sight of the royal palace.

The driver took an unexpected detour, skirting the town, and taking her off guard as he drove down a very narrow road that led to the back of the castle.

So, Natalia decided wryly, whilst her presence was commanded and so important apparently that she had been flown home in a private jet, her person was still unimportant enough to have to enter the palace via what looked very like much a tradesman's entrance to judge from its gateway—so narrow that she sucked in her breath fearing that the car was too wide to fit through it. Beyond the gateway lay a dank, unlit courtyard, the windows overlooking it were shuttered and the whole atmosphere was inhospitable and unwelcoming.

The chauffer had brought the car to a halt and was getting out to open the door for her. Despite her irritation, Natalia still managed to find a warm smile for him. He was after all merely following instructions.

This cloak-and-dagger type of thing was in many ways typical of the way King Giorgio ran his court, she thought ruefully. It wasn't unknown for those who knew him best to exclaim in irritated exasperation that Machiavelli ought to have been King Giorgio's middle name. The old king loved playing people off against one another, and always had done, Natalia acknowledged, but she admitted that she had come to feel a certain amount of sympathy for him as one after the other the candidates for his heir had had to be rejected. He might be arrogant and proud, but he was also old, and she suspected he had begun to feel real fear about what would happen to Niroli if he died without appointing his own successor. For all his faults, and she wasn't going to deny that they were many, no one could ever doubt his fierce love for his country. A love that she of course shared, as he well knew. He had surprised her once by telling her that she reminded him a little of his first wife, Queen Sophia, and that she had the same elegance and spirit. Natalia had been touched and flattered by his words, knowing how well thought of his first queen had been by the people of Niroli and those who knew her more closely. She suspected that it was in part because of this likeness to Queen Sophia that King Giorgio had initially conceived the idea of her marrying his newfound son.

A door was opening, a man coming towards her, although because of the lack of proper lighting she didn't realise that it was the King's Chief Minister until he reached her.

'Why all the urgency and secrecy? What on earth is going on?' she demanded.

'Come this way. I'll explain everything to you as I escort you to your apartment.'

Natalia, who had been on the point of walking into the palace, stopped and turned to look at him.

'My what?'

'Since you are about to be proclaimed as the official fiancée of King Giorgio's successor, it is only fitting that you should have your own apartments within the palace.'

'But I have my own home…'

'That is no longer suitable. Countess Ficino has been appointed as your personal lady-in-waiting. She will be responsible for the day-to-day organisation of your diary, and all matters relating to your wardrobe and your official duties. She will also be on hand to instruct you in matters of royal protocol.

'It is a pity that His Highness Prince Kadir has chosen to arrive ahead of schedule.'

'Prince Kadir is here? But I thought…'

'Exactly. However, it seems His Highness was so eager to make the acquaintance of his father and fulfil the promise he made to his mother on her deathbed that he gave into the impulse to arrive early.'

At any other time the stiff disapproval in the Chief Minister's voice would have amused her. The whole court operated under a routine so regimented and rigid that it was centuries out of date. Any hint of spontaneity was not merely discouraged, but actively stifled, and the prince would very quickly have been made aware of his crime in deviating from the agreed arrangements. Right now, though, she felt too irritated by the way her own life had suddenly been taken over to feel amused.

'The king fears that it will not be possible to keep his son's presence confidential for very long and for that reason he has brought forward both the official announcement of their relationship and of your betrothal.

'The palace's press officer has already alerted the media to the fact that a very important announcement is about to be made. That is one of the reasons why you were brought into the palace in the way that you were. Men are already working in the courtyard square in front of the palace decorating it ahead of tomorrow's speech from the king to present Prince Kadir to the people.'

'Tomorrow?'

The Chief Minister paused to direct her down a long corridor hung with gloomy portraits of past Nirolian heads of state. At the end a flight of marble stairs swept coldly upwards. At the top of them Natalia could see the familiar figure of the elderly countess waiting for her, her hands folded in front of her.

Natalia's brain was pulsing with questions but she knew there was no point in expecting answers from the elderly courtiers now flanking her. They were too steeped in the traditions of their roles to unbend enough to tell her for instance just what her husband-to-be looked like, and what kind of nature he might have.

Not that it sounded as though she was going to have to wait very long to find out herself, she admitted as she was handed over into the 'care' of the countess, who then escorted her up another flight of stairs and down another corridor to a pair of double doors.

'You will present yourself in the Royal Chamber tomorrow morning at eleven a.m. exactly. From there you witness the king making his official introduction of Prince Kadir to the people of Niroli from the salon adjoining the balcony. You will then wait fifteen minutes exactly before joining them on the balcony, where you will be introduced to Prince Kadir, and where you will both receive the king's royal blessing on your betrothal and forthcoming marriage.' She pushed open the doors to the 'apartment' inviting Natalia into the large salon that lay beyond them. Natalia's heart sank as she surveyed the heavy old-fashioned décor of the room. Three young women were standing with bowed heads, each of them dipping a curtsey in turn as the countess introduced them as her personal maids.

Natalia was used to managing her own staff, and she greeted each girl warmly in turn, asking them for their

Christian names. She could see that the countess did not approve of this informality but she ignored her disapproval. It was high time that the fresh air of modern life blew away some of the restrictions of court life.

'It is late, and you will of course wish to sleep ready for tomorrow, but first, it is my duty to tell you that the king has provided you with a new wardrobe to suit your new role, and I have given instructions to your maids as to which outfit you are to wear tomorrow for the official announcement of your betrothal.

'Additionally, I shall come to you just prior to you making your way to the Royal Chamber to ensure that everything is in order. I should warn you that whilst you are on the balcony the king intends to bestow on you some of the royal jewels that belonged to Queen Sophia. You will of course wear them as well during the formal reception that will follow the balcony announcements, but they are to be returned to me afterwards so that they may be put safely under lock and key.'

A new wardrobe; royal jewels. She should have anticipated something like this, but somehow she had not done so, Natalia admitted. It all seemed so outdated and ridiculous. She had seen the jewels worn by the king's second wife and she shuddered with horror at the thought of having to be weighed down with anything similar. It went against everything she believed in about the duty to help those less fortunate than herself to allow herself to be used as a display for so much wealth. It was one of her dreams that in time she might be able to influence her husband enough to persuade him to share at least some of the Nirolian royal family's fabled wealth with, not just Niroli's people, but all those people throughout the world who were in need. A charity to explore ways to develop better health care for everyone was just one of the things she would like to establish. It was things such as this that would be her reward for becoming Queen, not rows of diamond necklaces.

'I shall leave you now to prepare yourself for the morning.'

The countess made it sound as though she were about to go to the guillotine, Natalia decided ruefully, and perhaps in some ways she was. After all, her marriage to Prince Kadir would mark a very sharp slicing-off point between her old life and her new and it would certainly sever her from the sexual freedoms that belonged to a modern-day single woman. Why was she thinking that now? Not because of last night, Natalia hoped.

'If there is anything you should wish for,' the countess was saying, 'something to eat, a book to read perhaps, then one of your personal maids will be on hand to bring them to you.'

To *bring* them to her? What was wrong with her nipping out into the city and getting them herself? Natalia wondered independently as she thanked the countess and waited for her to leave. After all, for now at least she was still merely Natalia Carini and as such free surely to enjoy the anonymity of being just that.

The three anxious-looking young maids looked as relieved to be dismissed as she was to dismiss then, she thought wryly ten minutes after they had gone and she had her new apartment to herself.

Who had used these rooms last? she wondered.

Although the beautiful inlaid wooden furniture was polished and dust-free and every surface sparkled under the huge chandeliers, the salon still had an air of disuse and melancholy about it. Huge swathes of silk brocade covered the windows blotting out the light, and the same fabric had been used to cover the baroque-style gilded chairs and sofas scattered around the room. The colour of the fabric at least she could admire, since its sea-green-blue colour, under the light of the chandeliers, was only a few shades lighter than the colour of her own eyes. Natalia suspected it would originally have been chosen to reflect the colour of the sea, which this side of the palace would look out over.

A carpet replicated the intricate plasterwork design on the ceiling. A huge gilt-framed mirror hung above the fireplace reflecting the elegant proportions of the room with its matching pairs of double doors at either side of the opposite wall. One pair as she already knew led into the corridor, the other pair must therefore take her towards her bedroom.

Beautiful though this room was, it was quite simply not 'her'. She liked modern, pared-down décor, and simple natural fibres. She was fussy about what she bought, choosing only 'green' products, and just as fussy about sourcing them to make sure that the workers who produced them had not been exploited.

The small anteroom into which she had walked had another pair of double doors in it which as she had expected opened into her bedroom.

Her heart sank the minute she stepped into it. The décor echoed, indeed complemented, that in the salon.

A huge ornate French rococo-style bed was draped and swathed in the same silk, two further sets of double doors opened off it, both of them open. Through one lay a large bathroom with an enormous claw-footed bath, whilst the other pair led into a large wardrobed dressing room, which, as Natalia discovered when she walked into it, also had a door leading into the bathroom.

Someone had already opened and unpacked the suitcase she had brought with her from Venice. Behind these wardrobe doors lay the new clothes the king was providing her with for her new role. Trying to quell the horrible sinking sensation invading her stomach, she took a deep breath and opened the first pair of wardrobe doors. And then closed them again after one appalled look at the row of stiff satin evening 'gowns' and formally tailored silk suits—clothes far more suited surely to Queen Eva then they ever would be to her. Puce, jade-green, peacock-blue were not colours she favoured or that suited her, just as stiff tailoring was not her style. She thought longingly and rather angrily of her own clothes, soft, unstructured clothes in natural fabrics and colours that flowed round her body instead of constricting it.

She couldn't offend the king by refusing to wear what amounted to a gift from him, although she had no doubt that these garments had been chosen more with the dignity and image of the crown in mind than her feelings.

Those couture clothes with their intricate stitching and beading surely epitomised everything that she so passionately wanted to see changed about the monarchy and its relationship with the people of Niroli. In these modern times true respect surely came from having a monarchy that could be truly respected for the way the members of it lived their lives and cared for their people rather than being feared and admired for the power of their wealth and status.

CHAPTER FIVE

'MY SON…' King Giorgio murmured emotionally as he reached out to place his hand over Kadir's and shook his head in wonderment.

'Even now I still cannot believe it. It is like a miracle…' His expression changed, becoming harsh and stern. 'Your mother had no right to conceal your existence from me. But then that is women for you—enchanting creatures though they can be, they are not to be trusted to think or behave logically. It is a poor apology for a man, in my opinion, who allows a woman to rule him. But you, I can see, are not such a man, Kadir.'

Kadir could see the old king's emotions threatening to overwhelm him as he blinked and shook his head.

'To think that all this time when I had begun to despair of ever finding someone of my blood who was fit to rule Niroli after me, you should be there, the best and most suitable of all. My son…my son,' he repeated, clasping Kadir's arm firmly.

'Your mother did us both a great disservice in not revealing your true paternity earlier.'

His father's angry bitterness reflected his own feelings, Kadir admitted. In that as in so many other things—he was quickly coming to discover that he and the man who had fathered him were very alike. However, from the moment he had arrived at the palace, ahead of schedule, and not because of anything whatsoever to do with the woman who had so enflamed his desire in Venice, he had fought against picturing his mother here, a young virgin on her way to her marriage succumbing to the experienced sensual charm of the island's powerful King. These were not the mental images of his mother he wished to have, and so, like his unwanted memories of Venice, Kadir firmly refused to allow them space inside his head.

'Your mother would have deprived you of a truly great future if she had not acknowledged your true paternity,' the king was boasting.

'There are those who consider that becoming Ruler of Hadiya is a great future,' Kadir pointed out.

'Hadiya…' The king gave a dismissive shrug. 'How can ruling a few square kilometres of desert compare with ruling Niroli?'

'It is what lies beneath Hadiya's desert that gives it its wealth,' Kadir told him dryly. 'And there are many so-called rich Western nations who would sacrifice their pretty views for Hadiya's sands—and its oil.'

Kadir could tell that the king didn't like what he was saying, but he had no intention of allowing his newfound father to bully him. The late sheikh, his father, had been a powerful and autocratic ruler and one who commanded and indeed demanded obedience from all around him. Whilst his younger brother had accepted this easily and good-naturedly, Kadir had always fought against it and fought too to establish his own independence of spirit and outlook. He was not about to allow another autocrat to think he could rule him now at this stage of his life, even if that autocrat was his father, and, despite all his efforts to conceal it, growing tired and vulnerable.

'Here on Niroli when its crown is placed on your head you will be inheriting more than mere wealth,' the old king told him. 'You will be inheriting your true birthright.'

At forty he was surely old enough not to be swayed by such blatant emotional manipulation, Kadir told himself wryly, but there was a suspicious sheen of moisture in his father's eyes and a small tremor in his voice that threatened to undermine his own cynicism. Despite the king's outer shell of arrogance and disdain and his apparent lack of regard for those he considered to be of lower status than himself, especially the female sex, there was hidden within him some emotional vulnerability. Kadir was not easily swayed by the emotions of others, though. He had spent too many years concealing and even denying his own emotions to feel sympathy with emotional vulnerability in others. The truth was that he had spent far too long learning to protect himself by remaining 'apart' from society to abandon that defence system now.

It was in King Giorgio's interests, after all, to make him feel welcome and wanted. That did not mean the older man really felt like a father towards him. For the same reason Kadir did not allow himself to believe now that simply because King Giorgio was his natural father that meant that the people of Niroli would accept him with the same emotional delight as the king. Or that he himself would be able to feel the same sense of commitment and belonging that his father felt for his country. After all, he had not grown up here; as yet he felt no sense of kinship with it or with those who had.

What he did have, though, was the strong belief that here on Niroli he could put into practice the skills of government and diplomacy and leadership in his own way. His hope was that Niroli would give him the opportunity to stretch himself politically in the mainstream of the world arena in all the ways that Hadiya never could. And that in doing so he would find the inner peace and sense of himself that had previously always eluded him.

'Our people are already gathering in the square, crowding into it now according to the Chief Minister. They will welcome you, Kadir, because I, their King, am welcoming you, just as they will recognise you as their future King. All the more so, of course, when they learn that you are to marry Natalia Carini. I personally have chosen her to be your bride. She comes from an old Nirolian family, much respected on the island. Natalia lives and breathes Niroli; she will teach you all that you will need to know about the ways of the people. She is close to them and understands them.'

The picture his father was painting of his bride-to-be was not exactly one to stir a man to desire, Kadir thought cynically. Not that it mattered whether or not he desired her, just so long as he fathered a son on her.

Those were the rules of the game as he had grown up knowing it to be played and it did not concern him that he might not find Natalia Carini physically attractive. That was what a man who had to make a dynastic marriage accepted. He did, however, think it ominous that this father had not made any attempt to introduce them to one another prior to the imminent public announcement of their betrothal.

'I do not know how much time I may have left and for that reason, if no other, I have decided that your marriage to Natalia will take place in ten days' time,' the king told him. 'The arrangements for it are already in hand.'

Kadir frowned. He might have grown up in a royal household and indeed expected to succeed to its throne, but he was still not used to having such an important part of his life arranged for him in this autocratic manner, without being consulted beforehand. In Hadiya he would have had his own choice of bride, and not had one forced upon him.

'Won't the people find it somewhat suspicious that we rush into such a swift union?'

'If by suspicious you mean they might think you have already got her with child, then surely that would be all to the good. I know my people. There is nothing that will make them embrace you as their future King more eagerly than the birth of your son to a Nirolian wife.'

First marriage and now fatherhood, Kadir frowned.

'I still have certain duties I must perform in Hadiya, duties connected with the official handover of power to my younger brother, and which require my presence there.'

'That is easily dealt with. As soon as you are married you and Natalia can travel to Hadiya on honeymoon.'

Their conversation was interrupted as the Chief Minister came hurrying into the room.

'Your Highness,' he addressed the king, 'it is almost time. The people are already gathering, and Prince Kadir needs to change into the formal robes of state ready to be proclaimed your heir.'

'You don't really expect me to wear that!' Natalia stared in revulsion at the satin corset with its heavy-jewelled beading. It looked more like an instrument of torture than an article of clothing.

'The king specifically desires that you wear it. It is a copy of the gown worn by his first wife at her own betrothal,' the countess told Natalia stiffly. 'It is his belief that the sight of you in it will remind the people of their love for Queen Sophia and that they will transfer that love to you.'

And, of course King Giorgio, being the man he was, would never let slip an opportunity to trade on the loyalty of his people for his own ends, Natalia acknowledged disapprovingly, although in this instance she was obliged to admit that serving his own ends would also benefit his people.

The bodice of the gown had to be laced up so tightly that she could hardly breathe and then the straight, elegant column of its skirt attached to it. She had already endured an hour with a hairdresser summoned to put her hair up in a stiffly regal style and now as she looked at herself in the mirror the only familiar part of herself she felt she had to comfort her was the subtlety of her own specially blended scent.

There was a knock on the outer doors to her apartment and then they were opened to reveal the small phalanx of traditionally costumed palace guards.

It was time for her to go.

Once she walked through these doors she would be leaving Natalia Carini behind for ever.

When she walked back through them in her place would be the betrothed fiancée, soon-to-be wife, of Crown Prince Kadir of Niroli.

Kadir could hear the excited buzz of the crowd outside in the large courtyard below them. This room with its balcony onto the courtyard, according to his father, had been traditionally the place from which past kings had always addressed their people, giving them news both good and bad.

The doors to the balcony were hung with the Nirolian flag and the coat of arms of his father's family and that too of his mother's, and now those doors were flung open to a shrill fanfare of trumpets. As they stepped forward onto the balcony Kadir saw the rainbow-coloured ribbons of flowers and confetti being hurled into the air as the band in the square played the national anthem. The gaudy brilliance of the celebratory colours matched the excitement in the crowd as they yelled and cheered their joy.

He barely knew his father as a father; they were meeting now as two mature men both with their own agendas to promote. A fierce surge of unexpected emotion stabbed painfully through him, catching him off guard. He was forty years old, for heaven's sake, far too old and too self-aware to start mourning some sentimentalised vision of a non-existent father-and-son relationship.

King Giorgio stepped forward holding up his hands for silence.

'My people,' he announced. 'I give you my son.'

Natalia could hear the frenzied roar of the crowd as she stood in the shadows of the balcony room, waiting for her summons to join the king and her future husband. Down there amongst them would be her grandfather and other members of her extended family. No matter what other past quarrels might lie between them, her grandfather and King Giorgio were united in their love for Niroli.

Through the open doors she could hear the king's voice, trembling slightly now. With age? With emotion? His stirring words had certainly elicited a roar of approval from the listening crowd.

'We must always remember that there is a purpose in all things,' the king was saying. 'When one after another my heirs disqualified themselves from the right to follow me onto the throne, I was filled with despair, for you, my people, and for my country, not knowing then as I know now that fate had already chosen the one who will come after me; the son I did not know I had.

'A chance meeting many years ago led to his conception, hidden from me and kept hidden until his mother relented and confessed to him on her deathbed that I had fathered him. Prince Kadir has given up his right to rule the Kingdom of Hadiya to take on the mantle of his duty to his blood, my blood, your blood, people of Niroli. He will need help if he is to rule you as you deserve to be ruled and to that end it is my pleasure to inform you that my son, and your future King, Prince Kadir, will in ten days be married to Natalia Carini, daughter of Niroli.'

As the roars of approval surged upwards from the crowd Natalia felt the countess give her a small push. Automatically she took a step forward, and then another, her heart thudding frantically inside her chest cavity.

The brilliant sunlight after the shadows of the salon momentarily blinded her as she stepped out onto the balcony, trying not to wince at the shrillness of the trumpeters.

The king was standing in the middle of the balcony. She dropped him a small stiff curtsey and felt her bodice corset digging into her flesh as she did so. Behind her the court dignitaries were filing onto the balcony; below her the crowd was cheering and calling out her name exuberantly, 'Natalia. Natalia... You are a true Princess of Niroli.' The air was filled with the scent of the bombs of flower petals being thrown by the revellers, some of whom were already dancing to the impromptu burst of music from a lone musician.

'Daughter of Niroli,' she could hear the king saying firmly, 'give me your hand so that I in turn may symbolically unite it, and thus you, here in front of our people with the hand and the person of our chosen heir, my son Prince Kadir.'

The king was reaching for her hand, and for the first

time Natalia was able to look past King Giorgio and at her future husband.

The world swung dizzily around her as though she had been scooped up and were being swung from a funfair wheel. *Him! The man from Venice!* Leon Perez! Surely there was some mistake, and she was just imagining…but, no…it was quite definitely him! Prince Kadir, her husband-to-be, was Leon Perez, and the man she had made love with in Venice. It couldn't possibly be, but it was!

The shock struck right through to her heart, pinioning her with disbelief, sucking the air from her lungs and turning the bright sunshine dark. The sound of the crowd became a dull roar reaching her from a distant place. From that place she was only vaguely aware of the laughing excitement of the crowd being checked and then becoming a low-voiced sound of confused anxiety as they saw her sway and then semi stumble.

Natalia was oblivious to their concern. All she could see was the man who was to be her husband. He might be dressed in the historical dress uniform of the Commander-in-Chief of Niroli's Armed Forces, a cloak of dark green velvet lined with ermine slung from one shoulder, and the Nirolian Seal of State ring very evident on his ring finger, but none of that could mask the reality of the fact that he was the same man she had had sex with in Venice.

A hard hand gripped her by the elbow keeping her upright as she swayed, a too well remembered male scent shocking her senses. The murderous look he was giving her was enough to have her stomach lurching without his for-her-ears-only, 'Pull yourself together,' mouthed against her ear as he made a pretence of showing concern for her.

Somehow she managed to force herself to turn to the crowd and smile as the king placed her now-icy-cold hand on that of his son and heir, Niroli's future King and her future husband.

'My people,' King Giorgio announced emotionally. 'I give you my son and his betrothed, your future King and Queen. May their lives together be spent in joyful service to our country and may they be blessed with the gift of children to carry on our traditions after them. I ask you to pledge to them your loyalty and love, as they pledge theirs to you. My people, will you accept Prince Kadir as your future King and his wife-to-be Natalia Carini as your future Queen?'

'We will…' the crowd roared as though with one voice.

Their acceptance seemed to reverberate throughout the square as though sending its message to every part of the island, Natalia thought as she was overwhelmed by her own feeling of kinship with the people down below her in the crowd. She was a part of them and they of her in a way that the king and even less his son could ever be. She had been born amongst them and had grown up with them. She would, she promised silently, from now on dedicate herself to her service to them and to her country.

The crowd was now going wild with joy, some of the younger and bolder onlookers calling up to the balcony, 'Kiss her, Your Highness. Kiss your bride-to-be.' It was all Natalia could do to struggle to assimilate the true enormity of what was happening. How could this be? How could the man she had given herself to so ill advisedly in Venice be her future husband? She felt feverish and yet also cold, numb and yet acutely sensitive.

As though in obedience to the wishes of the crowd Kadir was leaning toward her. Instinctively she pulled back, as alarmed as though she were sixteen and a virgin and not twenty-nine and a mature woman. The hand clasping hers tightened its grip to an almost bone-crushingly punishing intensity, the green eyes sent her a message of warning and fury, and then the hard-cut male mouth was brushing hers to put a cold seal on the prison she herself had willingly walked into.

'One more thing,' King Giorgio was saying, as he had to raise his voice to make himself heard about the exultant roar of delight. 'In recognition of how much pleasure it gives us that Natalia should become the wife of our son, we wish to publicly make this gift to her.'

Somehow both the countess and the Chief Minister had managed to make their way to the front of the balcony carrying the leather-covered jewellery case, which they were now opening for the king.

The glitter from the sunlight reflecting on the diamonds inside it was so brilliant that it made Natalia's eyes hurt to look at them.

'These diamonds were my gift to my beloved first wife, Queen Sophia,' the king said emotionally. 'Since her death I have kept them locked away, unable to countenance seeing anyone else wearing them. Until now. Now it is my belief that it is fitting and right that they should now be worn by my son's betrothed, Natalia.'

Obediently she bent her head, shivering as she felt the cold, heavy weight of the diamond necklace lying against her skin.

'Kadir.' King Giorgio motioned to his son, indicating the enormous diamond ring that lay with the bracelets and tiara in the box.

As he picked up the ring Kadir looked at her again, his green eyes so hard with dislike and rejection that Natalia felt as if it were a physical blow.

'Let him give you the ring,' the countess snapped in her ear. 'The people will want to see you wearing it.'

Wrenching her gaze from Kadir's, Natalia held out her hand. Her fingers, long and slender, looked unfamiliarly delicate against the width of his palm and the length of his hand whilst the ring, held between his fingers, seemed to glitter malevolently at her. She was trembling so much that her hand brushed against him. Immediately he closed his fingers into a fist as though in rejection of the physical contact with her. Natalia's face burned. She longed for the courage to simply turn and walk away. But it was already too late. He was sliding the ring onto her ring finger, and holding up her hand to show the crowd.

The noise of their roared approval was almost deafening. King Giorgio was looking triumphant but she dared not look at Kadir to see how he might be feeling. Her heart felt heavy with the weight of what she feared lay ahead of her. But it was too late for her to have regrets now, she told herself sickly, before rallying to remind herself that she hadn't been alone in what she had done. But she had no explanation for what had happened; no rational means of making it seem more palatable. Unless she told him the truth. What truth? The truth that she had been so overwhelmed with desire for him that nothing else had mattered. Surely as her husband to be he would welcome that news.

CHAPTER SIX

WHEN was it going to end? Natalia wondered tiredly. She had not imagined, when the countess had told her that there was to be a formal reception after the announcements on the balcony, that she would have to stand at the side of her husband-to-be under such devastatingly untenable circumstances. Her head was throbbing and she could hardly move thanks to the constriction of her gown and the weight of the king's gift to her. It would have been bad enough if they had simply been the strangers they should have been and not...not what they really were.

There was no need for Kadir to tell her what he thought of her, those hostile looks he had been giving her had made it mercilessly plain, and yet what right did he have to judge her? What after all had she done that he had not? There was no point in her even thinking about trying to wave the equal-rights flag in this situation, though. In a marriage such as theirs there was all the difference in the world between the moral laws applying to the woman and those applying to the man.

Historically men of power and position married virgins on the assumption that way they would be guaranteed that the child born hopefully nine months after the consummation of the marriage would be theirs. The all-important first-born son. Despite the changes in the world over the last fifty years, the old beliefs were too deeply ingrained in some men to ever be erased or even softened. Kadir's heritage from his mother's people would mean that even more than most his pride would demand that the woman to whom he gave his name and his seed would be his alone. Natalia could sense that about him as clearly as though he had said the words to her himself. Her mistake was not so much what she had done, but that she had not thought more deeply about the expectations and mind-set of the man who would be Niroli's next King before allowing herself to be carried away on a wave of emotional loyalty to her country.

Theirs would not, she realised now, be a prosaic marriage of convenience between two people who understand one another's goals and beliefs. Even without Venice she would never have been the kind of woman Kadir would want as his wife. Her lip curled slightly in womanly contempt for a man she now saw as inwardly weak in all the ways that mattered the most to her, for all his raw masculinity and sexuality; a man who was so steeped in old-fashioned beliefs that he automatically considered it beneath him to take as his wife a woman who had been 'used' by another man.

She, on the other hand, was proud of everything that she was, of all that she had learned and all the ways in which she had grown from girlhood to womanhood by making her own choices and learning from them. Until Venice there had never been a relationship she had regretted or felt shamed by. She was a mature woman, morally the only judge she believed she needed, perfectly capable of policing her own sexual behaviour, instinctively knowing what was right for her and what was not. She had always believed that to deny her sexuality as she matured would have been as much of a sin as being promiscuous. And she wasn't promiscuous. How could she be when she had been celibate for so many years? The only time she had broken her own self-imposed moral rules—the only time she had ever wanted to, in fact—had been that one night with Kadir, but how could she make him understand and believe that, as she must—for the sake of their marriage and Niroli?

Here they were standing side by side as they greeted the guests invited to meet them, joined together by the king's own hand and by the heavy weight of the ring she was wearing, by the expectations of the Nirolian people, and yet in reality already divided by suspicion, deceit, mistrust and attitudes to life that were worlds apart.

Kadir could feel the stiff gold braid embossed collar of the uniform jacket he was wearing pressing against his flesh. It felt alien and constricting after the more familiar softness of the Arab robes he wore on formal court occasions in Hadiya, and more than that he felt almost as though he were dressed up to take part in a play, with a role imposed on him by the expectations of others, rather than living through a vitally important part of his own future life.

The research he had done on Niroli after his mother's devastating revelations had shown him an island with the potential to play a vitally important role on the world stage. Geographically alone, its position was unique. The world was changing; old powers giving way to new; men with minds sharp enough, perceptive enough, forward-thinking enough to encompass what could be achieved were in a unique position to guide that world through its rebirth. He had learned so much from studying the history of his own country and the Middle East in general. He wanted his future sphere of influence and that of his sons to reach far beyond Niroli, and to that end he had decided that he needed a wife who understood this, a wife who would dutifully provide him with children he knew would be his, not a woman who would casually give herself to any man who happened to stir her to lust—a woman who could be stirred to that lust as easily as a bitch on heat.

Kadir could feel fresh fury raging through him as he relived the moment on the balcony when his wife-to-be had stepped out to show herself. His wife-to-be was a whore...worse than a whore: *she* gave herself for nothing other than her own pleasure; a whore at least put a price on her virtue or lack of it. Every time he thought of the casual contempt with which she had disregarded their marriage to throw herself at him he wanted to turn to her and rip the diamonds from her neck and the ring from her finger, the clothes from her body, to reveal her as she really was.

How many times had she slipped away from Niroli to pose as she had done with him in a role that allowed her access to men? Ten times? A hundred? A thousand? How long had she planned to wait after their marriage before doing so again? A year…a month?

It was of course unthinkable that his father knew the truth about her. He had seen in King Giorgio's eyes the same arrogant pride he knew burned within himself. His father would never have considered her as a potential bride if he had known. The last thing he wanted to do was marry her, but the potential complications if he refused now were too great to be contemplated. He was the one who was the outsider here; the one who had to prove himself and win the acceptance of the island's people. To reject one of their 'daughters' would be seen as an insult, here just as it would be in Hadiya, no matter how justified his reason. No, he was stuck with the marriage if he wanted Niroli. And Kadir knew that he did.

The last of the guests were finally being persuaded to leave by the courtiers discreetly walking them towards the exit.

Kadir, deep in conversation with his father, was ignoring her. Deliberately? Did she need to ask herself that? The longer the reception had lasted, the more time she had had to think and to assess the stark reality of her future, and how impossible it was going to be for her to live it. She could see the countess coming towards her, no doubt about to suggest that it was time for her to 'retire', Natalia thought wryly.

Nirolian court etiquette remained firmly fixed in the habits of the early nineteenth century, where the men had to wait to 'let their hair down', as it were, until after the women had 'retired'. To judge from those left in the ornate grande salon now, with its décor and mirrors so very much in the style of the mirrored ballroom at Versailles the conversation amongst them would be very much on the future political strength of Niroli and its ruling Royal Family.

The countess had reached her and was waiting.

'What should I do about these?' Natalia asked her, briefly touching her diamond necklace.

'The king has made it plain that it is now your personal property,' the countess answered her briskly. 'It will make a good start for the jewellery collection you will need as Prince Kadir's wife. Of course, once he ascends the throne you will have access to the Crown Jewels of Niroli, and I dare say when he takes you to Hadiya with him after your marriage he will make a gift to you of his late mother's personal jewellery. Of course you can also expect to receive gifts of jewellery from the heads of other states and countries on your marriage, but for now, if you are ready to retire…'

Natalia nodded her head and then waited for the countess to escort her over to the king, so that she could go through the court formality of requesting his permission to leave.

He had just given this and to her relief turned his back to her, thus enabling her to turn round herself instead of having to back out of his presence, when Kadir broke off his conversation with his father to say curtly, 'I would like to have a few minutes private conversation with my wife-to-be.'

'Highness, provision has already been written into

tomorrow's schedule for you and Natalia to spend an hour walking together in public,' the king's Chief Minister began, but Kadir stopped him shaking his head.

'There are matters I wish to discuss with my betrothed that are for her ears only. With my father's permission I shall escort her to her apartment?'

King Giorgio actually laughed and gripped Kadir's arm, telling him jovially, 'You are a man after my own heart and indeed my son. I too would have wanted some time alone with my wife-to-be, in your shoes.'

'Your Highness, Natalia is still wearing Queen Sophia's jewels. She—'

'My son is hardly likely to steal them, Countess,' the king dismissed the countess's anxious reminder sharply. 'You have our permission to escort Natalia to her apartments, Kadir.'

The king had misunderstood the reason for the countess's comment, Natalia suspected, but then he had not had to wear the heavy jewellery and nor was he laced into a bodice so tight that Natalia suspected her ribs would be bruised when she was finally released from it. From the looks being exchanged by the remaining courtiers, it looked as though they and the king thought that Kadir planned to indulge in some pre-marriage intimacies, but of course Natalia knew better. Even so she didn't allow herself to betray her thoughts as she placed her fingertips on the arm Kadir extended to her, and allowed him to lead her towards the exit.

Already she was beginning to get used to the fact that her new role meant virtually always being surrounded by other people. Two uniformed guards snapped to attention as they left the grande salon, whilst a formally liveried attendant flattened himself against the wall of the corridor as they walked past him.

'My maids will be waiting for me in my room to help me to undress,' she told Kadir without turning her head to look at him. 'So whatever it is you wish to say to me, if you want to do so in private you had better speak now.'

'*Whatever* I wish to say to you? Isn't it obvious what I might want to say, or rather the explanation I might demand you give?'

'My behaviour before we met today as a couple about to enter into an arranged marriage has no bearing on that marriage,' Natalia told him quietly, hoping he wouldn't be able to guess that inwardly she was nowhere near as confident as she was trying to appear and was in fact feeling sick with guilt. 'You have no right to demand an explanation for it and neither do I intend to give one. I am mistress of my own life.'

'Mistress. You use *that* word with good reason. No wonder it slips so familiarly from your tongue. As easily as the lies you must have told over the years to conceal your true lack of morality. Had I known what you were…'

He wasn't making any attempt to conceal either his anger or his contempt and Natalia's body reacted to it, stiffening as she stopped walking and tried to pull away from him. Immediately his right hand clamped down on hers where it lay on his uniformed arm, imprisoning her as he turned towards her. She could feel his anger as though it had a life force of its own. His antagonism towards her filled the air around them, pressing down on her. They were alone in the corridor, no man had ever made her feel so physically vulnerable and *small*.

'What I am now is what I have always been, openly and honestly. My body is mine to gift as I see fit. My sole error, as I see it, was not in my desire but in my lack of judgement in my choice of partner,' Natalia burst out passionately.

'Of course you would have behaved differently if you'd known who I was.'

'That was not what I said and it certainly isn't what I feel. My lack of judgement was not realising how unworthy of me you are. You want me to feel shame, to allow you to blame me for some imagined crime against you that you consider I have committed. My crime, if there is one, is against myself, for not recognising how impossible it is for a woman of my outlook and independence to have any kind of relationship with a man like you.'

'You dare to speak so of me? You who have behaved as no woman with morals would ever behave.'

'No woman of morals? What do you know of a woman's morals? Nothing. All you know, all you want to know, of a woman is her obedience and her submission. A woman's morals are the pact she makes—the vow she takes for herself, with herself—and they rest in her alone. Only she knows where the defining lines lie for her and only she has the right to know. In the past my sexuality was mine to claim—for myself and for those I have chosen to share it. Our betrothal marks a point in my life where my "morals" compel me to consider my own desires in tandem with the restrictions placed on me by my soon-to-be public role as the wife of the future King of Niroli. In that role I have a duty to the people of Niroli and its Crown, and it has been my choice to accept that duty and those restrictions.'

'If you are trying to tell me that what I witnessed in Venice was a final fling, a sickening sexual binge intended to stifle your appetite for the rest of our marriage, then let me tell you now that I don't believe you. And even if I did, for me there would be no excuse—a woman who behaves as you did can never be a satisfactory wife or mother,' he told Natalia arrogantly.

It was too much.

'How very typical that you stand in sexual judgement of me. A woman's ability to experience sexual desire has no direct bearing on her ability to be a good wife and mother, far from it, and if you were half the man you obviously like to think you are you would know that for yourself.

'King Giorgio told me that you wanted to rule Niroli because you felt you could not in all conscience rule the people of Hadiya as you would have been expected to rule them. He said you wanted to embrace a more modern form of leadership. He said that you were ready to learn from me what it means to be Nirolian, but obviously none of that is true. And yet you have the gall to stand there and accuse me of deceit.'

In the shadows of the corridor she could see the warning angry colour seeping up under the taut flesh of his jaw.

'You dare to accuse me—'

'I dare to do whatever I have to do for my country. That is after all the only reason I am marrying you.' Natalia almost threw the words at him in defence of herself.

The look he gave her made her burn and now it was her turn to feel the hot surge of angry blood burning up under her skin.

'The only reason? What about the couture gown you are wearing, the diamonds around your neck?'

'You think I want those? Well, I do not. They mean nothing to me. No, that isn't true. What they represent to me is the way in which the poor are forced to work for a pittance so that the rich can adorn themselves. You talk of me deceiving you—well, I could make the same accusation of you. You are not the man I believed I would be marrying, the man I believed would be worthy of fathering my children.'

Natalia gave a small gasp as he took hold of her arm and wrenched her round into the light so that he could look down into her unprotected face.

'You dare to talk to me of the fathering of a child? Before this marriage of ours is consummated I shall require you to provide me with evidence that you are not carrying the child of another man.'

'That would be impossible since the last man, the only man in fact for a very long time, that I have been intimate with is you.'

'You expect me to believe that?'

'Why not when it is the truth? You are very quick to demand that I give you an explanation for my behaviour but you are just as culpable.' Natalia could see how little he liked her reminder. She was feeling so tired now and so emotionally vulnerable. A part of her was longing to be able to take hold of his hand and tell him how much she longed right now for the luxury of being able to be honest with him, and of being able to tell him that it was his own devastating effect on her that had led to her totally uncharacteristic need of him. Could she do that? Could she take that risk and beg him to give them both the chance of a fresh start, and one in which as his wife-to-be she was free to say openly how physically desirable she found him? They were to be man and wife, after all. Hope filled her. Surely it was worth her lowering her pride to ask him and to be honest with him…

'I am a man; it is several weeks now since I last spent any time with my mistress…'

He had a mistress. Natalia felt as though she had been plunged into a vat of icy cold water and held there until every bit of her burned with the pain of what she was being forced to endure. He had a mistress. Of course, he would. Of course he did! Why, why had she not thought of that simple explanation for his fierce possession of her for herself, instead of being foolish enough to imagine that he had wanted her for herself?

As though someone else had taken her over she heard her own voice saying with brittle emphasis, 'Really? Well, I am sure she will be delighted to learn that you haven't allowed yourself to suffer any sexual frustration whilst you've been apart from her.'

Kadir cursed himself under his breath. Why had he allowed her to infuriate him into saying anything about Zahra, especially when their relationship was already over? Kadir had his own self-imposed personal moral code and it did not include having sex with a mistress when he was a newly married man. Somewhere at the back of his mind there had been the intention of establishing at least a working sexual relationship with his bride, even whilst he had also realistically acknowledged that it was all too likely that there would not be any real passion or desire between them.

How fate must be laughing at him for the trick it had pulled on him. There was no way he could establish a comfortable sexual relationship with this woman, whilst when it came to passion and desire… He did not feel passion or desire for her. Logically speaking it was all too likely that he had been driven to possess her in the way that he had because he had been living a celibate life. That was all. Nothing more. Nothing personal… Nothing that meant that he had actually wanted her so much that that need had overridden everything else.

That intense, unbearable pain inside her couldn't really be because Kadir had told her he had a mistress, could it? It mustn't be. Not now that she knew what he really thought of her. She could not, would not, endure a marriage in which she wanted a man who felt only contempt for her. She could not take the risk that that might happen and there was only one way she could ensure that it did not. A quick slicing shaft of swift agony now to separate her from him for ever and it would be over, leaving her free to make her own life, if necessary away from Niroli. That would bring more pain—she loved her country so much—but she must not think of that now. Natalia took a deep breath.

'Look, why don't I save us both from a situation neither of us want?' she told Kadir briskly. 'I've changed my mind, Kadir, and I do not intend to marry you. I shall tell the countess in the morning and ask her to inform—'

'No!' The vehemence of his own denial shocked through him. 'No,' he repeated. 'You will do no such thing. You will marry me and you will do as I say.' Not because he wanted her. Never that. No, it was for Niroli and the future that she had to be his wife. King Giorgio had rejected many heirs already; Kadir wasn't about to give him a reason to reject him.

'This is Niroli, not Hadiya,' Natalia told him angrily. 'You may have been proclaimed as Niroli's Crown Prince, but there is no rule of absolute royal law here. Niroli is a democracy; we have laws that protect the rights of the people. Enforced marriage does not happen here.'

'You will marry me.' Kadir continued as though she hadn't spoken, 'because if you don't, I shall tell the world that I am the one who is refusing to marry you because of your behaviour.'

She was trapped, Natalia acknowledged bitterly. She might not care what he told the world for her own sake, but she did care for her grandfather's. He would be shocked and hurt and, not just that, he would feel publicly humiliated, as well.

'You will marry me and from now until the day you conceive my child I do not intend to let you out of my sight. I will make sure you are watched day and night to make sure that you are never given the opportunity to foist someone else's bastard on me. Since it is necessary for me to have heirs, you had best hope that you conceive as quickly as possible—once our month of abstinence is up, that is. I need to make sure you aren't carrying someone's bastard.' He released her so abruptly that she almost staggered into the corridor wall, her arm throbbing where the blood was returning to it.

CHAPTER SEVEN

NATALIA looked unhappily round her bedroom. Later on today Kadir would make his formal oath of allegiance to Niroli and King Giorgio and in return the king would proclaim him Crown Prince. Tomorrow morning she would be married to Kadir in Niroli's cathedral, and then the next day they would board the private jet taking them on their honeymoon journey to Hadiya.

Tonight, as on every night since their engagement had been announced nine days ago, two guards would be on duty outside both exits from her apartment. It was a formality Kadir had somehow or other managed to persuade the countess was necessary. During the daytime there was never a minute when she was left alone. Either the countess, or one of her maids or, even worse, Kadir himself was at her side. The countess had told her that Kadir was concerned that her new duties might prove too onerous for her and so had asked the countess to be on hand at all times to help her. The maids seemed to think that without them in attendance she would not be able to manage the lavish couture outfits Kadir had insisted he wanted to see her wearing in preference to her casual clothes, clothes which in their way were as constricting and imprisoning as any lock and key. And then there were those worst of all times when Kadir would put his arm through hers, the gesture of a devoted tender fiancé asking her to walk in the palace gardens with him so that she could acquaint him with the history of the Nirolian people.

Part of her, the weak part that she privately despised, longed for her to get pregnant as soon as possible so that she could escape this constant stifling monitoring but another part of her, the real, stronger part of her, hated the thought of her bringing a vulnerable child into the world under such circumstances, and longed to find a way to escape from her marriage.

On their return from their honeymoon they would be sharing the royal apartments traditionally made available to the Crown Prince, and in a few minutes' time she was due to make a tour of them with Kadir and the Comptroller of the Royal Household. Was this what she had given up her freedom for? This marriage based on suspicion and mistrust to a man she now felt she despised as much as if not more than he so obviously despised her, and certainly far more than she had ever wanted him? How foolish the high-minded ideals that had motivated her to agree to marry Kadir seemed now. How empty the promises she had made to herself of what she would do for her husband and their people.

'So when was the last time these rooms were decorated?'

It surprised Natalia that Kadir should ask such a

question. It seemed out of character for him to concern himself with something so trivial.

'They were last decorated for occupation by the king's late son and his family.'

Did that explain the air of sadness that seemed to haunt the now-empty rooms? Natalia wondered. The king's first-born heir, Queen Sophia's son, had after all died in tragic circumstances and prior to that there had been the trauma of the kidnap of one of his twin sons.

The remaining twin, Prince Marco, might be happy now married to his English wife, Emily, but he had freely admitted that his childhood had been shadowed and difficult and that he had as an adult felt alienated from his birthright. So much so in fact that he had rejected the throne. She had no wish for her children to suffer the same fate. The burden of royal birth could be a heavy one if it was not lightened by love and the closeness of a shared family life and sense of purpose. She wanted her children to grow up in the sunshine of Niroli's future with their hearts attuned to that future and the way in which they would share it with the people of their country.

The room they were in had windows that opened out onto a private inner courtyard garden on one side, and the sea on the other. Impetuously Natalia turned to the comptroller, addressing him directly for the first time.

'Are there no rooms we could have that have windows overlooking the city?'

The comptroller was frowning. 'There are such rooms, yes, but traditionally members of the royal family have preferred an outlook that gives them privacy.'

'What is it you have in mind?' she heard Kadir demanding, as though impatient of her input.

'Our children will one day be the ones to take Niroli forward into the future,' Natalia informed them both. 'How can they do that if they grow up turning their faces away from our people? How will they understand and appreciate what it means to be of Niroli if they never see how our people live? As a child I roamed the city freely, exploring it, making it my own, binding it to me as it bound me to it. I could find my way through its streets blindfolded, I know now every nuance of its scents, all the places where the most precious flowers and herbs grow. Loving a country is something a child learns from its parents. Understanding it, knowing it and its people is something they can only learn by experience.'

She had said too much, been too outspoken, Natalia recognised, and in doing so would of course have antagonised Kadir and harmed her cause.

'It is for His Highness to approve or disapprove our apartment,' she told the comptroller tiredly. 'I must be guided by what he says.'

'My wife-to-be is right. I myself know now little as yet of my new country. A man who looks only inward learns much of himself but little of others. A king who would rule others must learn to study them as well as himself. If there are rooms available with windows that overlook the town...'

Natalia stared at the comptroller in disbelief. Kadir was agreeing with her, supporting her. A seed of something fragile but, oh, so precious was opening inside her heart beneath the warmth of her pleasure in his reaction, and putting out small quivering tendrils of hope. She turned to look at Kadir, but he was looking away from her.

'It is also my wish that my wife and I share a bed instead of occupying separate rooms,' Kadir was telling the comptroller in a businesslike voice. 'After all, we have a duty to provide Niroli with the next generation of heirs.'

'The state of marriage is so approved by God as to be the foundation of family life where children are born...'

Natalia tensed under the heavy weight of her ornate wedding gown and long veil. The Valenciennes lace overdress of her gown had originally been made for Queen Sophia's wedding dress. Softly cream with age, it looked magnificent over the shimmering gold dress beneath it.

It had always been Natalia's intention not to wear a white gown. She was a woman not a girl, a woman proud of all that she was. And if Kadir was not man enough to accept that, if he had felt it necessary to turn to her and give her a look of comprehensive cynicism when she had joined him at the altar, then that was his choice. Her conscience was clear.

Was it? If she should have conceived in Venice... *If* she should have, but how could she have done so when Kadir had used protection?

Kadir's white uniform with its gold braid, instead of looking faintly ridiculous, actually brought home to her the reality of what it had meant in previous centuries for a king and his heirs to ride out into battle for their country at the head of their armies. All too easily she could see Kadir in such a role. Not that Hadiya or Niroli had been at war during Natalia's lifetime, and nor would she want that. In fact she hoped that she and Kadir and then through him their children would play a strong role in promoting world peace. So why did she find it so stirring to visualise him in a combatory role? Women were drawn to the alpha men their instincts told them could protect them and, more importantly, their young, Natalia reminded herself as she forced herself to look forward instead of towards him.

'I pronounce you man and wife…'

Natalia was shocked to discover that she was having to blink away emotional tears as the notes of 'Ave Maria' soared from the choir to fill the ancient cathedral and Kadir raised her fingertips to his lips.

It was done. She was his wife. Her commitment to her country and its future must now come before everything else.

Natalia was now his wife. This woman whom his intellect told him to despise and revile but whom his body ached for in the dark, empty hours of the night. Where had that admission come from? Kadir wondered grimly. So there might have been one night, possibly two when he had woken up like many another man with his body aching for a woman—that hardly meant that he desired Natalia Carini. Not Natalia Carini any more but Crown Princess Natalia, he reminded himself. His wife, his partner in this new venture he had committed himself to, a decision he'd probably made to avoid acknowledging his difficult relationship with his father.

How old had he been when he had first realised that the man he had believed to be his father did not love him, and that nothing he could do would ever draw the praise from him that he so willingly gave to Kadir's younger brother? Eight? Six? Younger? Old enough to recognise he was being rejected certainly and at the same time still young enough for that to hurt, and for him not to have known how to put in place any defences against that pain. How could his father have turned away from him, his eyes cold and his manner aloof, whilst they had lit up with warmth the minute his gaze had rested on Kadir's younger brother, his manner changing to become paternally indulgent?

He could still mentally see and sense his mother's anxiety as she had stood watchfully in the shadows of the courtyard where he and his brother played. The minute his father had entered the courtyard a word from his mother had brought a maid to his own side, a firm hand on his shoulder as he had been led away, leaving his parents alone with his brother.

His protests had always been met by some rational explanation: he was the elder, and had his schoolwork to do; his brother was just a baby. And he had struggled harder to win his father's attention and approval whilst his mother had in turn worked harder to keep them apart.

'I did it for your sake,' she had told him. 'To protect you because I was afraid that he might look at you and see as I could see so clearly that you were not his child.'

All lies of course. She had not done it to protect him but to hide her shame and protect herself. But as he had come to learn, that was what women did. They lied to protect themselves and then added insult to injury by pretending that their motivation had been altruistic. A man did not allow women to undermine him. He certainly had no intention of allowing Natalia to undermine the position he intended to claim for himself here in Niroli. It was all too easy now for him to understand why his father had so often, and unfairly, he had believed at the time, questioned Kadir's own allegiance to Hadiya and his ability to rule it well. His mother had sworn to him that her husband had never known he was not his son, but Kadir was not convinced. The sheikh might not have been able to prove he hadn't fathered him, but Kadir felt sure that he had had his suspicions. He had seen by example what happened between man and child when that man did not accept his paternity of that child. That was not going to happen to him. No child growing up with his name would ever have cause to doubt his love or his complete belief that he had fathered him.

They were to spend the first night of their marriage in their palace apartment before flying to Hadiya in the morning, and Natalia stood stiffly still and silent in the middle of her large dressing room whilst her maids removed her ornate gown. Whatever the circumstances she would have felt some natural apprehension about what lay ahead tonight. She might be old enough not to be sentimental about human sexual relationships, but she would be lying if she tried to pretend to herself that there wasn't still a tiny part of her that foolishly longed to experience the close intimacy of a loving sexual relationship in which the two parties concerned were totally committed to one another, and that it hurt knowing that she would never have that.

Despite that she had determinedly refused to think of herself as a daydreamer or an idealist, but now she knew that her biggest mistake had been in believing that she and Kadir would bond over what she had believed would be their shared commitment to Niroli. Taking due care to make their relationship work would surely mirror the care they would take to work for the higher good of the island. That mind-set seemed risible now in view of what had happened. She thanked her maids as she stepped out of her gown and then scooped it up, acknowledging how bitterly disappointed she was and how bitterly angry with herself—and Kadir—she felt.

Beyond her dressing room lay her private bathroom just as on the other side of their shared bedroom lay Kadir's dressing room and his private bathroom. She really didn't want to think about the preparations he might be making for this, their first night together as the future King and Queen of Niroli. Was he still determined to wait a full month after Venice to consummate their marriage? Surely he would come to her on their wedding night?

She was under no illusions and knew that he had meant what he had said about having her watched night and day until she had conceived his child. How bitterly ironic it was considering her long years of celibacy. A celibacy broken only by her overwhelming desire for one man— Kadir himself.

She had already made it plain to her maids that she

preferred to bathe alone, and her eyebrows rose when she walked into her bathroom and saw the champagne chilling in a bucket of ice. To calm her bridal nerves? Whose idea had that been? She would have preferred a glass of Niroli's organic white wine, given the choice.

She showered quickly and efficiently instead of luxuriating in the huge round bath, drying herself and then pulling on a towelling robe to make her way to the bedroom.

Someone had been in to turn down the bed and switch on the beside lamps, and another ice bucket had been placed close to the bed.

She stared at the empty bed and then took a deep breath and pulled back the covers to get into it and wait for her husband.

Two hours later she was still waiting. She had heard sounds from Kadir's dressing room, the murmur of voices, probably his valets, she guessed, and then silence, and now as she released her muscles from their bonds of tension she acknowledged the unwantedly unpalatable truth. Kadir did not intend to spend the night with her and she would not be spending her wedding night with her new husband, but on her own.

Had she been nineteen his behaviour might have reduced her to a tearful, quivering, shamed wreck of rejection. But she wasn't nineteen and she certainly didn't intend to let Kadir play mind games with her and win. And that ache deep down inside her? What ache? She refused to allow there to be any ache, she decided proudly.

CHAPTER EIGHT

NATALIA had thought she knew heat, but Niroli's heat was nothing compared to the hot blast of air that had greeted them on their arrival in Hadiya. It had been like standing in front of an open oven door with a fan blowing.

Here though, at least, in the private apartments she had been assigned in the women's quarters of the Hadiya Royal Palace, the architecture made the most of what breeze there was, especially in the beautiful courtyard garden.

She had woken this morning breathing in the scent of the roses from that courtyard, whilst her ears were filled with the gentle sound of falling water and the fan of the whirring wings of doves. Every aspect of the apartment was designed to fill the senses with delight, right down to the coffee she was now drinking as she sat admiring her surroundings and considering everything that had happened following their arrival in Hadiya the previous night.

If she was honest it had shocked her to see just how very Eastern in its customs Hadiya actually was. There had been no question of her attending the formal reception that was given to welcome Kadir home as the Crown Prince of Niroli. Instead she had had to watch the proceedings from behind the delicate grill work that separated the women's area from the public 'divan' Kadir's brother was holding.

It had also seemed strange to her that Hadiya's subjects were in theory free to attend such a 'divan' and ask questions of their ruler. The young woman who had been appointed as her guide in matters of Hadiya protocol had carefully explained to her that in these modern times all those wanting to approach the sheikh were carefully vetted first. It was a custom much like that of the traditional 'laying on of hands' common amongst European monarchs.

It was certainly potentially a very democratic process, making the ruler approachable and accessible to his subjects from all walks of life. And one from which Niroli might benefit?

A slightly wry smile touched Natalia's mouth now. She doubted that many brides of two days' duration would be spending their time thinking about matters of political domestic policy, especially not when they were married to a man as outwardly physically sexually attractive as Kadir. But then not many new brides would have spent all those nights sleeping alone.

It certainly wasn't a part of Hadiya protocol for newly married couples to sleep alone and apart. Basima had already discreetly let her know that it was considered perfectly proper and indeed expected for a bridegroom to visit his bride in those rooms set aside for her.

'It was the sheikh's wish that you should be given the apartment of his mother, the sheikha,' she had explained that first evening, and for a few minutes Natalia had thought she was telling her that it had been Kadir who had requested his mother's rooms for her, but then she had realised that Basima was telling her that it had been Kadir's brother, the kind and jolly new sheikh, who had requested that the rooms be prepared for her.

And what of the haughty and arrogant woman who had been introduced to her as the daughter of a prominent Hadiyan—Zahra Rafiq? What a wonderful thing the female instinct was. Natalia had disliked her intensely even before the other woman had let her know very unsubtly that she was Kadir's mistress. Was? Zahra had certainly made it plain that she wanted that relationship to continue, but Zahra lived here in Hadiya and, as Kadir had already made clear to Natalia albeit in a very different context, he considered his future role as Niroli's King of first and foremost importance to him, above and beyond everything and everyone else.

Had Kadir spent last night with Zahra? Her hand shook, making her put down the glass perfume bottle she had been given in Venice and which some impulse had made her bring with her to Hadiya.

She had watched whilst Zahra had prowled her room, picking it up herself. Somehow it had not surprised Natalia to see the way the beautiful glass had dulled the moment Zahra's fingers had tightened around it. No wonder Zahra had replaced it so swiftly, looking at it with scorn. She on the other hand loved the way it glowed at her touch, giving off a warmth that seemed to heal the sore places of her heart, reaffirming for her that she was the worthwhile human being she knew herself to be. Now she put the bottle down.

Logically speaking, why after all should it bother her if Kadir had a mistress and that mistress was Zahra? But a person's emotions weren't always subject to logic, were they? Was she just a jealous wife resenting another woman's role in her husband's life? Since when had her *emotions* had any role to play in her marriage? They didn't, and they must not, Natalia told herself fiercely. Just because she had felt physical desire for Kadir that did not mean that emotion was involved. Right now she was going to forget that she had ever had this time-wasting conversation with herself, and focus instead on her new role as consort to Niroli's Crown Prince.

This morning, for instance, she was going to be given a tour of Hadiya's new technical college for girls, an innovative step towards modernisation set in motion by Kadir's mother, where young women could learn modern business skills. The outer door to the room opened and, as though her thoughts had had the power to produce her like a genie from a bottle, Zahra herself stalked in. The lushly curved socialite with her dyed blonde hair was the kind of woman instantly recognisable to other women as cold and calculating and yet somehow perceived by men as being sweetly feminine and desirable.

'I have told Basima that I shall accompany you on your formal visit this morning,' she announced. 'There are matters I wish to discuss with you that will be of benefit to you in your marriage to Kadir.'

Natalia gave her a long thoughtful look, and then reminded herself of the decision she had just made.

'I doubt it,' she told her calmly. 'A mistress's experience of a man rarely has any bearing on his wife's experience of him. The role of a wife after all encompasses so much more than merely spending a few hours in his bed giving him pleasure.'

Natalia could see from the flash in Zahra's hard brown eyes that her own deliberately pointed comments had hit their mark.

'Kadir is right. You are not the kind of woman he would have married had he remained here,' Zahra returned with a falsely sweet smile. 'But of course we all know that the only reason *you* have been elevated to such a position is because of the folly of Kadir's mother. Had she not compounded her sin of betraying her husband by keeping the truth of Kadir's paternity to herself then there would have been time for Kadir to make more suitable arrangements for his marriage.'

'I am not surprised that Princess Amira found it necessary to keep her secret, given the lack of understanding she was likely to have found,' Natalia retaliated quietly. 'But if by more suitable you are thinking of yourself…'

Natalia could tell from Zahra's swift and audible intake of breath that she hadn't been prepared for her to be so outspoken.

'I am far too modest to dare to dream of such an honour.' Zahra told her, sounding anything but modest. 'It is enough for me that Kadir is generous to bestow his loving desire on me.'

Just so long as it came with a huge helping of expensive gifts and public recognition of the importance of his mistress's unofficial role, Natalia decided cynically.

'For me Kadir's happiness is far more important than my own,' Zahra continued unconvincingly, 'and that is why I am forcing myself to put aside my natural feelings in an effort to help you to become the kind of wife Kadir needs.'

Zahra was clever, Natalia admitted. Zahra wanted a fight and she certainly knew how to provoke one, there was no doubt about it. With those few well-chosen words she had well and truly ignited the slow burning fuse of Natalia's own sensitive temper.

'Look,' she told her curtly. 'Let's not waste one another's time. Why don't I be blunt? Kadir has chosen to accept an offer put to him from the King of Niroli, *my* country, not Kadir's and certainly not yours, to become its next King; a role which he is only eligible to play through the mother you seem to despise so much. King Giorgio has chosen *me* to be Kadir's wife because, whilst I may know now nothing of the customs of Hadiya, I do know the hearts and the minds of the people of Niroli. I know what matters to them, how they think and how they feel, what they want in their new King and what they don't, because I am one of them. That is why King Giorgio asked me if I would consider giving up my personal freedoms as a single woman to become the wife of Niroli's future King. It is out of love for my country and my duty to its future that I agreed. A large part of that duty as Kadir's wife is to make sure that he is kept aware of the needs and beliefs of his adopted people.'

Let Zahra think about that! She was not going to allow Zahra or anyone else, but most of all Kadir himself, get away with thinking she was some docile obedient fool, dazzled by the false glitter of a royal title; someone so shallow and lacking in substance that she could be bribed with it into accepting the bullying of her husband's mistress. Natalia had her own agenda for her future as a royal wife, and it certainly wasn't for the royal title that she had agreed to marry Kadir.

'I don't need you to tell me that his marriage to you was not of Kadir's choosing,' Zahra interrupted her angrily. 'Do you really think I do not know why Kadir did not come to you last night?'

Now it was Natalia's turn to suck in a breath as sharply as though she had sucked on the fruit of one of the lemons growing on the trees outside in the courtyard.

'You talk very cleverly about the practicalities of your arranged marriage, but you cannot deceive me. I can see into your heart and what you want to conceal there. You want Kadir as a man.'

Natalia felt the words as though they were physical blows. They weren't true. They couldn't possibly be! She wasn't going to let them be. Kadir meant nothing to her. *No? Then why had she behaved the way she had in Venice?*

That had had nothing to do with wanting Kadir. She had just...

She had just what—just wanted sex?

Yes!

No! Because if that were true then why had she been able to spend so long living her freely chosen celibate life so comfortably?

She had been celibate for too long, that was all. Kadir could have been anyone.

Liar—isn't it the truth that the moment you saw him you felt…

I felt nothing, she denied furiously. Nothing. And she continued to feel nothing for him now despite what Zahra was trying to say.

'Did you really think I would not know?' Zahra continued to taunt her. 'Kadir and I have laughed about it. Kadir has his duty to perform, of course, but it is to me that he gives his true passion. I am the one who will sit beside him when ultimately he rules both Niroli and Hadiya. It is my destiny to be with Kadir, not yours. Kadir is mine and I will never let him go. Nor will I ever let anyone or anything come between us, and you had better remember that. It is our destiny to be together,' she repeated, 'and nothing can stand in the way of that destiny.'

How had it happened that suddenly their argument had veered off the apparently straight road at such a sharp angle that it had completely thrown her? The conversation had taken a completely new and disturbing direction, Natalia realised, remembering the intensity she could hear in Zahra's voice.

Listening to Zahra, Natalia was suddenly struck how very similar in attitude Zahra seemed to be to the kind of woman the press delighted in labelling a 'stalker'. But maybe she was being unfair and jumping to the wrong conclusions. Maybe that was the way a passionate Middle Eastern woman spoke? If so it certainly contrasted with her own far more pragmatic approach to life, Natalia admitted. Zahra must of course know that there was no way Kadir would ever succeed to the Hadiyan throne. After all Kadir had already renounced the throne of Hadiya. Zahra was something of a bully, Natalia guessed, and no doubt used to frightening others into giving way to her. Well, she was going to have to learn—and Kadir with her—that she was not bullied so easily. Far from it.

'You are beyond foolish if you think that Kadir does not see as I do that for all your pretence not to, you yearn to give your heart to him.' Zahra astounded Natalia by throwing the accusation at her, and in doing so changing tack yet again. 'How predictable you are to fall in love with him as you have done. I told him it would be so. How indeed could it not be with a man such as Kadir? But he does not want your love; he does not want anything of you. Why should he when he has me, and when he will always have me? I am the one he loves and he will never give me up…never.' Zahra moved closer to Natalia and then unexpectedly grabbed hold of her arm before Natalia could move out of the way. Her nails were long and lacquered a blood dark red. 'Do you understand that?' Very determinedly Natalia stood up, ignoring Zahra's hold on her.

'I understand that if I don't get ready now I shall be late for my formal duties,' she answered her as lightly as she could.

What nonsense Zahra had talked. As though she would be foolish enough to fall in love with Kadir. She was a mature woman, not some foolish young girl with daydreams. If she believed in romantic love, and Natalia was not sure that she did, then she still felt that a couple needed far more to build a life together on than merely 'falling in love'. They needed shared beliefs, and shared interests, a shared sense of commitment and dedication; they needed of course the passion that came with mutual sexual desire to truly have the foundations of a long-term relationship, but sexual desire could not be relied upon to last and was surely the least important of all those 'must haves'.

'I want to talk to you.'

'Well, I do not want to talk to you,' Natalia snapped back smartly at Kadir as he followed her into her rooms dismissing the waiting maids with a curt inclination of his head.

'That is something you have already made more than evident today,' Kadir retaliated sharply as the maids melted away leaving him to slam the door enclosing the two of them in the dimly lit room.

In the time it had taken them to walk through the palace from the cars, darkness had fallen. They had just come from the final formal event of that day, the opening of a new shopping centre, attended by not just the two of them but also Kadir's brother and his wife and family. The glass doors to the courtyard were still open and Natalia went to stand in front of them to breathe in the rose-scented air. The car in which she had travelled had reeked of the strong Arabian perfume favoured by Zahra. Natalia could smell it coming off Kadir now.

'What was there for me to say?' she challenged him. 'Your mistress pre-empted every attempt I made to speak.' She wasn't going to let him see how angry and then humiliated she had felt at the way in which Zahra had upstaged her or how foolishly hurt she had been about the fact that she had not had the opportunity to use the few words of Arabic she had so carefully learned and rehearsed so that she could greet the children in their own language. To do so would make her seem petty, and reinforce Zahra's accusation that she was emotionally vulnerable to Kadir, which she wasn't; not in the least! Not now and not ever. Zahra was welcome to him in that respect. In *that* respect maybe, but Natalia, in her role of consort to the Crown Prince of Niroli, did not intend to continue to allow herself to be humiliated the way Zahra had done, for the sake of Niroli itself.

'Why bring Zahra into this?' Kadir demanded angrily. 'She has nothing to do with it.' It had thrown Kadir completely on his return to Hadiya with his wife to find Zahra insisting on behaving as though they were still lovers. He fully intended to discuss her behaviour with her and remind her that their relationship was over.

'She has *everything* to do with it,' she contradicted him. 'You may think that by foisting your mistress off on me as my official Hadiyan female companion it is only me who is insulted, but you are wrong. What you did insults the Throne of Niroli as well because it elevates your mistress to a superior position than me, your wife. This is not what King Giorgio had in mind when he agreed that I should accompany you here.'

'You dare to lecture me on my behaviour? You dare to question my decisions on matters of protocol and diplomacy?' Kadir was practically incandescent with fury, Natalia recognised. '*If* Zahra *is* my mistress.'

'*If?* There is no "if" about it, is there, Kadir? She told me herself this morning exactly what she is to you. Your mistress may feel she has the right to pass on to me her expertise on the subject of how best to act as your consort so as to make the best impression on you and the people of Hadiya. However, you are not becoming King of Hadiya, but King of Niroli, and it seems to me that she is in danger of making the same mistake as you and that is in believing that Niroli is some kind of extension of Hadiya, simply because you want it to be. Your word is not law, Kadir, and my guess is that you have already found that out here, but because you cannot accept it you have blamed your mother for your own inability to adapt to become the ruler Hadiya needs. If you aren't careful you will repeat that mistake on Niroli. The more I learn about your mother, the more I wish I had met her. How brave she must have been and how saddened and disappointed that you, the son she did so much to nurture and protect, should be so lacking in vision and so filled with self-delusion and bitterness that you cannot see her for the wonderful loving and giving person that she was.'

'Why, you—'

Kadir was looking at her as though he wanted to lock his hands round her neck and choke the life out of her, Natalia recognised, but she didn't care. If he hadn't had the decency to protect their marriage and his new wife from the venom of his mistress, then he could take the consequences. She looked across at him. The lamplight revealed Kadir's features quite clearly. She could see the harsh down-turned curl of his mouth and the cold glitter of anger in his eyes.

'You hate this, don't you?' she challenged him before he could finish. 'You hate being married to me. Well, you only have yourself to blame.' She saw the flash of temper igniting the jade-green darkness of his eyes.

'I am to blame for your immorality?'

He was as adept as his mistress about changing the direction of a conversation to suit his own ends, Natalia acknowledged, but she was not going to give in to those tactics.

'The fact that you have chosen to think me immoral does not make me so. And what you are to blame for is insisting on marrying me when you have already judged me to be not good enough to be your wife. You are angry with me, but in reality your anger should be for yourself.'

'How typical of a woman that you use words with the same deceit with which you use your body.'

'There is no deceit apart from in your imagination,' Natalia rejected his accusation.

'Have you forgotten the wanton way in which you, a woman on the brink of marriage, gave yourself to me?'

'My physical desire for you had no bearing on my commitment to this marriage. As a single woman, which I was, I had the right to own my own body and my own desires, and besides…'

Just in time Natalia managed to stop herself from admitting that he was the only man she had given herself to in a very long time.

'And as your husband-to-be, I had the right to expect you to bring yourself to our marriage bed free of any evidence of another man's possession of you. I will not be cuckolded in the way that my mother—'

'But there isn't another man! And it always comes back to what happened with your mother, doesn't it?' Natalia retorted. 'You can't move forward into the future, Kadir, because you will not let go of the past. Your mother was eighteen,' she told him grimly, already protective of the young girl who must have suffered dreadfully and been so afraid. A true man, a loving son, surely would have compassion for her and understand how she must have felt. But it was not Kadir's mother she wanted to discuss. 'You talk of my supposed immorality. That is so hypocritical when you yourself have a mistress. And by the way,' she added cuttingly, 'the next time you feel like discussing my failings as a wife with that mistress, I suggest you at least tell her that you've already had sex with me.'

'What do you mean the next time I feel like discussing you with my mistress? What are you talking about? Tell me!'

'Tell you? Yes, I will! Zahra couldn't wait to let me know that she knew I spent last night alone. You're a fine one to talk to me about morality. And, no, I didn't descend to her level and spoil the fun she was having letting me know how wonderful you think she is in bed by telling her that I already know that by my standards her idea of fun isn't anything to write home about.'

'You must have misunderstood her,' Kadir stopped her curtly. 'I did not spend last night with Zahra.' Kadir could hardly believe what he was admitting, and he certainly did not know why he was admitting it.

'Oh, come on, you don't really expect me to believe that, do you?'

Ignoring her, Kadir continued coldly, 'I spent last night in the desert. My brother had made arrangements for us to visit the tomb of our mother together.' His voice had become clipped. 'It was her wish that she was buried with her parents. We spent the night there together in prayer.'

Something—shame, perhaps; regret maybe—fierce and scalding burned its way through her, but she couldn't let it sway her.

'You cannot deny that she's your mistress, though.'

Kadir's eyebrows rose. 'You sound more like an emotionally jealous and possessive traditional wife than someone taking part in an acknowledged dynastic marriage.'

Kadir's criticisms were so close to what Zahra had said to her—so close that it was obvious to Natalia that they had shared a discussion about her and her supposed 'feelings' for him. What had they said? And where? In the intimacy of their shared bed? And no doubt when Kadir made love to Zahra he... The pain seized her out of nowhere shocking her rigid; leaving her unable to either fight it or deny it. If she had any sense she would abandon this discussion and now before it got totally out of hand, a warning voice inside Natalia's head urged her, but she refused to listen to it. Her pride was hurt and demanding recompense for the wound inflicted on it.

'My concerns are exactly the same as your own,' she told Kadir furiously. 'On health grounds alone, you must see that you can't expect me to share your bed when you are having sex with another woman.'

She saw from the faint widening of his eyes that she had caught him off guard, but he recovered very quickly, telling her coldly, 'I wasn't aware that I *had* asked you to share my bed.'

'Good, because although Zahra may consider you to be a good lover...' she began insultingly.

'You do not?'

How had he managed to get so close to her without her noticing him moving? Too close, she recognised uneasily. 'No, I do not! But then of course my experience of you as a lover can hardly compare to Zahra's, can it?'

What was she doing? What was she saying? She might as well throw herself off the top of one of Niroli's cliffs, her behaviour had become so self-destructive, Natalia recognised.

'If that is meant as a request for me to remedy that disparity—' Kadir began.

'No, it is not.' Now look what she had done, fool, fool that she was!

'Of course a woman like you will not be able to go very long without hungering for the feel of a man between her legs.'

She did not deserve so cruel and cutting an insult. 'A woman like me?' Natalia's eyes flashed a stormy petrol-blue-green.

'You know nothing about women like me. How could you? Zahra is your image of what a woman should be; everything about her is fake, from her dyed hair, through her faked submissiveness, to her no doubt faked orgasms,' she threw at him passionately, and then stopped as something in his silence told her that she had gone too far.

'Keep away from me,' she protested apprehensively, backing away from him. 'Don't touch me.'

'I am your husband. I have the right,' Kadir reminded her silkily.

'Keep away from me,' Natalia repeated. 'You…you stink of her scent,' she told him wildly. 'It makes me feel sick.'

'With what? With jealousy?'

There it was again; that accusation that made her heart jump around so painfully inside her chest.

'No! Why should I be jealous of a relationship I would not want, and will never want, even if you went down on bended knee and offered it to me? I am your wife and it is my duty to have sex with you.'

'Your duty? You mean like it was your duty in Venice,' he taunted her.

He was circling her like a hawk circling its prey, Natalia acknowledged. Even the unmoving air in the room felt heavy and weighted with the promise of implacable determination to make her back down. She had pushed him too far, Natalia admitted, dangerously too far, and for what reason? Because Zahra had got under her skin?

'So let us see then—again—just how good you are at separating duty from desire, shall we?' Kadir told her softly.

No woman had ever aroused him to such passion and fury, to such a fierce, consuming need to make her take back the lies with which she had ripped apart his pride. Right now the only thing that would salve his wounds would be her tears of regret and shame as she begged him to forgive her. And then begged him to possess her?

'You will take back each and every one of those insults before tonight is over,' he told her savagely as he reached for her.

CHAPTER NINE

NATALIA lay still on the wide bed, her heart thumping visibly heavily within her naked body. She would not demean herself by trying to resist. Physically his strength was the greater, and all that she wanted now was for him to leave her alone, even if to have that she had to allow him to inflict his hunger for punishment on her first.

Kadir could feel his heart hammering against his ribs. In the lamp light her skin was the colour of clear warm honey. Just seeing her was awakening an unsteady mental flash of jumbled images of the last time he had seen her this intimately; images he had had no idea until now that his brain had even recorded, never mind put to a sound track of his own arousal and spliced with the scent and the feel of her until the images sprang to unwanted three-dimensional life inside his head in a way that under-mined his self-control and fed his hunger for her.

She had challenged his maleness in a way he could not leave unanswered. And that was the reason he was doing this. The only reason. There was no other. She herself meant nothing to him.

* * *

Kadir's hands shaped her body, mercilessly seeking to expose its weaknesses, Natalia sensed. His touch was light and gentle and far too knowing. It skimmed her throat and then her breastbone, the curve of her waist, the shallow dip of her belly and then began again. She badly wanted to draw in a huge lungful of air, but she dared not let him see that need in case he took it as a sign of weakness. His fingertips stroked the delicate flesh just behind her ear. A shudder racked through her body. Because of the chilling night air coming in from the courtyard, Natalia assured herself, nothing more. And that heavy, expectant weight of sensual awareness mushrooming low within her body? It was nothing. Nothing at all. Less than nothing. She could quite easily pretend she couldn't feel it. Quite easily. Couldn't she? She could feel his mouth against her skin, the tip of his tongue sliding expertly against the sensitive ridges of her ears. Why did he have to do that to her? How did he know…? Her whole body shuddered as though it had been electrified as she tried to fight her own pleasure and failed. She put out her hands to push him away, but he caught hold of them, forcing them back onto the bed, his fingers locked around her wrists, leaving his mouth free to torment her agonised flesh as he trailed slow, fiery ribbons of unbearably erotic stimulation from one sensitive point to the next and then the next, each tug on those ribbons drawing the ache between her legs tighter.

When his tongue-tip flicked against the tight heart of her nipple she cried out like someone in mortal agony, begging him to stop.

'Are you sure? Wouldn't you rather I did this?' he tormented her, brushing her nipple with his lips, releasing her wrists so that he could cup her breasts and then tug rhythmically on her flesh making her whole body respond to that rhythm.

Tears of disbelief and despair stung her eyes. How could she have let this happen so easily? She wasn't a girl to be overawed by her own body's needs. She had felt like this before.

Had she? Had she, or was the truth that she had never known anything like this, or anyone like this? No! She would not let herself think like that.

If it was the truth then she could not and wouldn't admit it, and never wanted to know it again, Natalia told herself as she fought desperately to stave off her own defeat. Never!

He should be celebrating winning; he should be exulting in his victory over his ability to bind Natalia physically to his will, Kadir knew as he felt her losing her self-control and being forced to submit to her desire for him. Only he wasn't celebrating, Kadir acknowledged; he could not do so because with every touch, every stroke, every kiss, every breath of his body, his senses were playing out too much of the reel of his own self-control. He was no longer controlling her sexual desire, instead it was controlling him. As if they were two finely opposed and equally balanced powers, all that was supporting the edifice he had built out of her desire and his own fury was the counter weight between them; if that broke he would be plunged into the abyss of his own desire for her. He must stop now, withdraw from the field, leaving her punishment for her offence incomplete even if that meant that he had to go without the full taste of her complete surrender on his lips as she begged him for his possession of her—and he withheld it. She must never know he felt like this, ached like this and needed like this. It broke all the rules of what he was, so carefully constructed to protect him. The rules he'd created as he'd grown up with a father who had rejected him and a mother who had seemed not to care, a first young love to whom he had given his trust and his infatuated adoration and who in turn had betrayed him; they had taught him not to be ruled by his emotions and not to trust those who tried to touch those emotions.

Now unexpectedly all that was in danger of being undermined by a woman who had the power to move him to such anger, to excite him to such desire, to wound him to such depths that all of him that was male clamoured within him to compel her to sacrifice herself to him in payment for that sin in every way that there was. But somehow things had rebounded on him.

He would stop now before it was too late. Now, after just one more touch, just one more kiss, just one more heartbeat imagining the shuddering, gut-wrenching pleasure of her hands on his body, and then…

Natalia clung to him, her nails biting into the smooth warm flesh of his upper arms, her head falling backwards as she arched up in sensual sacrifice.

The scent of her would live with him for ever, ever constant and yet ever changing with each breath she took, one minute cool and aloof, another hot and charged with her arousal. It filled his senses colouring even the taste of her when he folded back the swollen lips of her sex to draw from her the fierce pulse that lay within the moist heat of her body. Now of its own accord that hard bead of flesh pulsed and throbbed, her body eagerly opening to the stroke of his fingers. He could do it now, stop and walk away letting her know the price she must pay for what she had said. He *could* do it, but the feverish movements of her body were more than his own could bear. The ache he had thought controlled had become a raging, savage, primal male call he couldn't silence or ignore.

Had it been like this before? If so she couldn't remember it, Natalia thought feverishly as her clitoris quivered with orgasmic shudders of moist urgency and the muscles within her flexed helplessly against their own emptiness. She had never wanted like this before; must never, ever want like this again. It was killing her, destroying her, taking her down to a dark place she was afraid she might never come back from out of fear for what it was doing to her and what it might turn her into. She heard a raw moan. Her own?

No. It was Kadir's male voice savage with a need that her own senses recognised as he moved over her and stroked into her, full and hard, momentarily satisfying the greedy contracting of her muscles as they clung avidly to him, relaxing into helpless pleasured obedience when he commanded their movement. The pleasure running swiftly through her was now gathering pace, climbing swiftly, mounting the plateau and going way way, beyond it, taking her with it.

Kadir's breathing was a harsh litany of command and

demand against the ear, her body tightened fiercely around him in a series of sharp contractions. She could feel him starting to withdraw, instinctively she clung to him, until she could feel the hot, wet pulse of him inside her.

Too late…too late! He had left it too late, but Kadir couldn't see any sign of triumph in the glazed darkness of Natalia's open-eyed gaze as he looked down into her eyes.

CHAPTER TEN

THERE WAS NO denying the fact that Natalia had a way with her that people responded to, Kadir admitted as he watched from a distance whilst she thanked the suddenly shy school children who had gathered in the square outside the palace of Niroli to welcome them back. He had seen it in Hadiya when she had talked to the women there, communicating with them despite their inability to speak one another's language. Somehow she had reached out to them and made them laugh and respond to her, just as the children were doing now. His mother had had the same gift. His mother!

Kadir withdrew from his own thought as though it had physically burned him. Natalia had had no right to speak to him about his mother as she had done. She knew nothing of their relationship or of his childhood. And as for her gibe about him wanting to prove himself to his mother's husband, the sheikh—that was so much rubbish. What did he have to prove? He had chosen voluntarily to hand Hadiya into his brother's care after all.

He had not slept with Natalia for the last two nights

they had spent in Hadiya. To punish her or to prove to himself that he controlled his desire for her and not the other way around?

'My son—I have missed you! It is good to have you back.' King Giorgio's greeting was warmly emotional as he welcomed Kadir with these private words during the formal reception ceremony to welcome them back. Was it his imagination or was his father's handshake really not quite as strong as it had been? Kadir felt an unexpected pang of emotion grip his heart as he looked at the older man. There was nothing to link them together other than their blood; no shared past, no shared history, and yet his father's words touched a place deep within his heart.

'We have so many years to catch up on,' the king was saying. 'May God grant me enough time. What I wish for more than anything else now, Kadir, is to hold your son in my arms; the next generation. Niroli's future King, born here of my blood and of the blood of the island through Natalia.'

The king looked across to where Natalia was still talking to the children. 'Kings cannot always marry where they wish, but in Natalia you have a wife perfectly suited to her role. When I look at her I see both my gentle first wife Queen Sophia and your own mother, she has qualities that belonged to both of them.'

One of the smallest of the children surrounding Natalia was accidentally jostled by some of the others and started to lose his balance. Kadir watched as Natalia saw what was happening and acted promptly, scooping the little boy up to give him a cuddle whilst exchanging a few words with his mother. Immediately the child's threatening tears turned to shy smiles, and it was obvious to Kadir how at home he felt in Natalia's arms, and how easily she had diffused what could have been a difficult situation. But it wasn't her unintentional display of her skills as his future consort that was causing that sharp shaft of pain to lance through his heart, was it? A sense of something breaking open inside him under intense pressure filled his body and his senses. It was a physical pain accompanied by a surge of melancholy; a feeling of loss and aloneness and angry antagonism and a profound sense of longing.

He had no need to ask himself what was happening to him. He knew all too well that the protective shield he had thrown around his emotions had cracked apart. Because of Natalia? Because she was making him both see and feel things about his own behaviour and his own reactions that he couldn't ignore? He didn't want this. He didn't need it and somehow or other he was going to make sure he found a way not to let it happen.

'Now,' he could hear the king saying, 'whilst you have been in Hadiya our Chief Minister has been putting in hand the arrangements for your formal ascension to the throne. There is much we need to discuss.'

Although she was refusing to look at him, Natalia knew the minute Kadir left the square with his father. She could almost feel the empty space where he had been just as she could feel the emptiness beside her in bed at night where he should have been. Had he shared Zahra's bed in Hadiya when he had left her alone in hers? The violence of her own jealousy filled her throat with nauseous bile.

What was happening to her? This was not the way things were supposed to be. She and Kadir were supposed to have a calm, adult, businesslike relationship based on mutual respect and awareness, on a shared desire to work towards an acknowledged logical goal, a relationship within which there was trust in their commitment to that goal, and trust too in their mutual awareness that nothing outside their relationship should prejudice it. Their marriage was supposed to be one where both of them retained the right to their own emotions and ultimately to their own freedom sexually—so long as they were discreet—where they wished. So how had this happened, how had she been turned into a seething mass of furious female jealousy at the mere thought of Kadir so much as looking with desire at another woman? Was Zahra's accusation true? Had she fallen in love with him? If so, no wonder she was feeling so sick and dizzy.

'And the funds we receive from the charitable trust set up by Prince Marco and his wife enable us to provide the very best kind of neonatal care, and to attract top experts in their field to our hospital.'

The young Chief Administrator was beaming with pride as he showed Kadir and Natalia over the newly opened wing of Niroli's maternity hospital, which they were visiting.

As she listened to the administrator Natalia risked a brief glance at Kadir, wondering how he was reacting to this mention of King Giorgio's eldest grandson whom he had not as yet met and who should have been the one to step onto the throne when the old King stepped down. She could not, though, see any hostility in Kadir's concentrated expression of interest as he listened attentively to the young administrator. No, it was more *her* sex—or at least certain members of it—that aroused him to anger, she acknowledged as she stifled a small yawn. Not because she was bored, but rather because she was feeling so unusually tired for some reason.

'Thanks to the charity donations, we have been able to acquire for our maternity unit two of the world's most up-to-date foetal scanners. These machines are capable of taking three-dimensional pictures of the unborn child—thus enabling doctors to pinpoint any potential problems far earlier than was previously possible.' The administrator showed them some example images.

Natalia was reluctantly being forced to admit that Kadir was handling his new role with far more sensitivity and diplomacy than she had expected. At no time during the last few hectic days of tours around government institutions, factories, vineyards and the like had he ever by so much as the flicker of an eyebrow displayed anything other than complete understanding of and respect for the obvious pride of his new subjects in their country; never once had he mentioned Hadiya or offered any comparisons between the two countries, never once had he risked offending the pride of the old guard, whose stiff formality on first being introduced to him had quickly melted into open respect for him once he had listened to them. And yet he still showed them what kind of King he was going to be with informed questions, and crisp forthright answers to those questions they put to him once he had broken down the natural barrier of their reserve towards him as a stranger.

'He is King Giorgio all over again and more,' Natalia had heard one of the village headmen saying approvingly. 'He is a true man and not afraid to say what he thinks. Mark my words, he will rule Niroli as it should be ruled.'

'And the young people of Niroli are saying that it will be a true new beginning for them and that we shall no longer be left in the past when our new King takes the throne. King Giorgio has been a good king, but he is the king of our grandfathers and our great-grandfathers, he's getting old and he no longer goes out amongst the people as Prince Kadir is doing, talking to them and learning how they feel,' one of her young maids was telling Natalia excitedly as she helped her to remove the heavy formal gown she had worn for the evening's reception to introduce Kadir to the most influential of Niroli's citizens and some from the international community of the very rich who owned property on Niroli, along with the resident diplomats from other countries.

Kadir needed no help from her in speaking with such people nor in subtly using his skills in diplomacy to persuade them that the future of Niroli was one they would be privileged to both invest and share in, Natalia had recognised. She felt a small pang of regret as she felt her own role was diminishing in a direct ratio to Kadir displaying his leadership skills. After all, the whole purpose of her agreeing to marry Kadir had been her belief that she was doing so for the benefit of her country. Now it seemed that Kadir might not need her help as much as she had believed, and that he was perfectly capable of winning the love and the respect of the people by himself.

And, as though that weren't enough, to judge from the snatches of conversation she had overheard, the evening's event had secured a large number of pledges from the super wealthy to assist Kadir in his plans to take the island into the kind of future that would benefit, not just those who invested money in this, but also the people of Niroli themselves.

'The greatest investment of all will not be the money you pledge to the island, but rather the investment made by the people of Niroli when they return your investment to you tenfold with the skills our young people will be able to learn with your financial support and co-operation.'

Natalia was not surprised that Kadir had received a standing ovation for his speech.

'Everyone is saying how fortunate we are to have such a handsome Crown Prince,' her maid confided as she removed Natalia's heavily beaded gown. 'They say that you will make very beautiful children together.'

The Crown Prince might be handsome, but what she longed for was a true marriage. Her new life might be busy, but right now it was leaving her feeling hemmed in and restless, she admitted as she thanked her maid and dismissed her. Because she envied Kadir the many challenges that lay ahead of him? Because tonight she had seen so clearly the breadth of the vision he had described so well to those listening, and she had longed so fiercely to be his true partner in that vision? His true partner in every single way?

That could have been, perhaps if only he had not judged her as he had. Now of course he saw her as a person he could not trust. They could have had so much together, worked so closely together. Natalia blinked away the pain given tears clouding her eyes and went in her bathroom.

Tonight, as he had done every night since their return to Niroli, Kadir would emerge from his own dressing room to share their huge bed with her, but he would not touch her. Not now. Not until she told him whether or not the intimacy they had shared had resulted in a child. Natalia placed her hand to her still flat stomach. She had first suspected the truth the morning of their return flight from Hadiya, but she had had to wait until she had gained the privacy of her grandfather's home and the services of the old family doctor who was her grandfather's close personal friend and sworn to secrecy to confirm those suspicions. The tell-tale line in the pregnancy-testing kit the doctor had given her had confirmed what she had suspected—she had conceived Kadir's child. The dates also confirmed that this child, this son or daughter, had *not* been conceived after their marriage in Hadiya, but in Venice. But how, when he had used a condom? It was hardly a question she could ask her family doctor. All she could do was assume that the condom had failed as she now remembered reading somewhere that they weren't a hundred per cent effective.

Perhaps because of the concern of her own thoughts she had lingered longer in her bathroom than she had intended with the result that Kadir was already in bed when she returned to the bedroom.

Kadir slept naked, and she knew it was that knowledge that caused her heart to jerk sharply as she tried not to see the way the light from the bedside lamp played on the smooth olive tautness of his shoulders and chest as he lay propped up against the pillows reading a document, and not the fact that she was concealing from him something he had every right to know.

Kadir watched Natalia approach the bed. She was wearing a thin silky robe that, whilst concealing the feminine curves of her body, somehow still drew mental images for him of a highly sensual and intimate nature.

'I have to thank you for the role you played in the success of tonight's reception,' he told her as she sat down on the edge of the bed with her back to him, discreetly slipping out of the robe before getting into the bed.

'I was only doing my duty,' Natalia told him woodenly.

Immediately his mouth thinned and he put down the papers he was holding.

'I would strongly advise you against adopting the role of a martyr,' he told her. 'It does not suit you. You are an extremely intelligent woman well versed in world affairs, with an important role to play in the future of Niroli.'

Natalia stared at him, astonished that he should compliment her.

Kadir was a proud man, it wasn't easy for him to admit that he had made any kind of error of judgement, never mind a huge misjudgement, but he was also a formidably fair and honest man. He had watched Natalia today interacting with their guests during the formal reception. He'd seen just how valuable an asset she was going to be to him and to the future of Niroli. He had been surprised and impressed today at the ease with which their separate roles had harmonised, thanks to Natalia. He had watched her speaking on a one-to-one basis to several of their male guests and at no time had her body language been anything less than confidently professional. She had not flirted, or teased; she had not used the obvious sensuality of her body or her beauty to focus their attention on her. Instead she had held them captive with her intelligence, winning their respect with that air of calmly regal distance he had watched her adopt in public. That they were charmed by her was not in doubt, that they would envy him such a wife so openly and obviously, he had always known, but that she should by her manner know exactly how to ensure that she was treated with the respect her role demanded had surprised him. Even if no one had introduced her to anyone within that room today as Niroli's future Queen, everyone there would have guessed it from her dignified warmth. Natalia possessed that rare ability to be both genuinely herself and what others expected of her. He looked across at her as she lay next to him all too aware of the now-familiar ache that wanting her brought to his body. They were married, their future lay together, he wanted her, and he knew he could arouse her to desire for him. Maybe these were the things he should concentrate on instead of focusing on her sexual past?

Natalia reached out to switch off her own bedside light, tensing a little when Kadir did the same.

'Don't let me stop you from reading your papers,' she said lightly.

'They can wait. Right now I have far more pleasant duties I prefer to perform,' Kadir told her smokily, catching her off guard as he reached over to her.

Wasn't it poor, unloved Catherine de Medici who had desperately refused to tell her husband that she was already pregnant because she longed so much to be intimate with him and to keep him in her bed and out of that of his mistress? Natalia thought guiltily as she felt her body flooding with response to the deliberate intimacy of Kadir's actions.

'Perhaps I should be grateful that fate has given me a wife so easily stirred to passion,' he murmured.

The trouble was that it was no longer merely physical passion he aroused in her, Natalia admitted as she shivered with pleasure beneath the sensual play of his fingertips against her naked flesh.

'Natalia...'

It shocked her to feel the warmth of his breath so close to her lips, and it shocked her even more to recognise that he was going to kiss her. The intimacy of shared kisses had not after all been something that had played a role in their relationship. The sweetness of eager, hungry kisses belonged to lovers and they were not and never could be that. And yet her lips were parting on a small exhaled breath, and then softening beneath the persuasive hard warmth of Kadir's. How easy it was to wrap her arms around him now and to pretend that this was a new beginning for them, a chance to start again. How easy and how very foolish and yet she couldn't stop herself from doing so as she melted into his hold as the intimacy of his kiss deepened from slow, masterful exploration to a fierce possession that had her heart thudding against her chest wall.

'Natalia… My wife…' Kadir whispered softly against her lips as he threaded his fingers through her hair and held her still beneath him.

'My wife… My Queen…' He kissed her slowly and lingeringly, making her shudder with female longing for what was to come. He kissed the corners of her mouth and then traced its outline with his tongue tip.

'Your perfume is as permanently etched into my senses as the perfume of life itself. I breathe it in with every breath until I am constantly filled with the memory of you, but tonight you are not a memory, you are a reality…' His tongue thrust against the frail barrier of her lips, deliberately taking possession of the inner sweetness that lay beyond them, stroking against her own tongue until he had seduced it into begging to reciprocate his intimacy.

Natalia could feel her head spinning. This was like no intimacy, no kiss she had ever known before. It was unique, overwhelming, possessing her…branding her as his for all time.

'There were many at the reception today who let it be known that they expected us to make haste to fill the palace nurseries and provide Niroli with a new heir, but none of them are quite so persuasive as my father,' Kadir told her. 'He reminded me only the other day that he may not have much time left to him…'

Natalia went cold as she listened to Kadir and realised just why he had initiated this intimacy.

Of course he was only making love to her because it was his duty to do so, and she was a fool if she had thought anything different. If? Why was she bothering to try to deceive herself? She had responded to him, welcomed him in her arms as a woman welcoming the man she loved. Had Zahra been right after all? Could she have seen what Natalia herself had not wanted to see?

'What is it?' Kadir was asking her. 'What's wrong?'

She couldn't bear to have him guess the truth and realise what a fool she had been. Bearing his contempt was hard enough; she didn't want to have to bear the burden of his pity as well.

'Nothing,' she told him lightly. 'I am sure that King Giorgio would admire your dedication to your duty.'

She was mocking him, Kadir realised angrily. Had she guessed that just now when he had touched and held her that the only kind of duty he had been obeying had been his duty to show her just how much he desired her? Just as other men had desired her and possessed her before him. Men whom she had loved? Did she think of one of them when he held her in his arms just as his mother had thought of her lover and not her husband, secretly longing for that lover whilst obeying the 'rules' imposed on her by her royal marriage? Did every prince with a kingdom to inherit share this bitterness he felt at the thought of being tolerated, endured by the woman to whom he was married because of what he was? And what was it exactly that he wanted? He was forty, not a boy—he had long ago become cynical about the reality of 'love'.

Why was he experiencing these contradictory feelings that were pulling him in two such completely opposite directions? It wasn't necessary for him to share any kind of emotional intimacy with Natalia, and therefore it wasn't necessary for him to be feeling what he was feeling right now. Maybe not, but he must have absolute loyalty and fidelity in his wife. He must be able to trust her moral stature, knowing the pressures their position would put on her, and he was a fool if he didn't recognise that a woman who had so easily given herself to him on a mere whim did not have that moral stature, no matter how much he might wish to convince himself that she did. It wasn't for his own sake he must remember this, it was for the sake of his role as Niroli's future King. If he knew that Natalia could be not trusted, then he knew also that she must be morally policed to ensure that she did not bring disgrace on the crown and a bastard child into the royal nursery. Giving in to his desire was not policing those morals, it was indulging himself. Trying to convince himself that he might have been wrong about her was the worst kind of self-indulgence there could be for a man in his position, and he must not do it. He must not let her think that he had any weakness for her. Angrily he crushed the unwanted and unnecessary tender feelings that had come from nowhere to challenge the reality of their relationship.

'I can assure you that no one will be happier to abandon that dedication than I,' he told Natalia harshly. 'You cannot surely think that I have any real personal desire to possess you.'

His words cut into her like a razor and in the agony of

her emotional pain Natalia didn't think of the consequences of what she was saying when she told him recklessly, 'Well, you may as well abandon it right now, then.'

There was a small ominous silence and then Kadir was reaching up and switching on his bedside lamp so that he could look down at her.

'And what exactly does that mean?' he demanded.

'It means that I am pregnant,' she told him quietly. It was too late now to wish that she had been more cautious.

Kadir started to frown. 'That is good news, of course,' he told her formally, 'but isn't it too soon for you to be sure…?' Here thankfully was a way out of his impasse, at least for the duration of her pregnancy.

Here was her opportunity to backtrack and lie by default by accepting the get-out he was unwittingly offering her. What difference would it make, after all? She knew that this child she was carrying was his. A baby born a matter of about two weeks short of nine months would not cause any undue comment, and there was surely no point in risking what she knew she would be risking if she told Kadir the truth.

But how could she lie to him feeling about him the way she now knew that she did? She already knew how little he trusted her sex; she was not his mother, a young girl forced by fear and circumstances to foist her lover's child on her husband; this baby was after all Kadir's. She did not want the baby or their marriage to be shadowed by the burden of any kind of deceit. Who knew what the future might hold or how close to one another the years might one day bring them? It was perhaps foolish of her to have such dreams, but she did have them and she could not bear to prejudice them by building into the foundation of their future now a deliberate lie.

As though her silence had alerted him to the truth, Kadir's frown deepened. 'When?' he demanded curtly. 'When was this baby conceived?'

Natalia took a deep breath.

'In Venice,' she answered him. 'I conceived in Venice.'

To her shock he thrust back the bedclothes and got out of the bed.

'Kadir!' Natalia protested.

Her admission coming so closely on the heels of his own private thoughts felt almost as though they had been some kind of warning omen. If so it was one that he could not afford to ignore.

'That is impossible. We used protection, as you very well know.'

'I know you did, but condoms aren't always infallible,' Natalia pointed out. 'They do occasionally fail.'

'How convenient for you, but I don't accept your argument, not having had firsthand experience of your promiscuity. What happened, Natalia? Did you allow a lover to be over-enthusiastic and then decide that you had better ensure that you had sex with me, as well, just in case you might be carrying his child? Did you deliberately seek me out in Venice, knowing perfectly well who I was? After all, I have used my polo playing alias for many years now.'

Natalia gave a gasp of shocked disbelief.

'That's ridiculous,' she told him shakily. 'I had no idea who you were and there was certainly no previous lover. I don't—'

'You don't what? Have sex with strangers?'

Natalia could feel her face starting to burn. There was no way she could defend herself from that charge.

'Nothing you can say to me will convince me that the child you are carrying is mine,' Kadir told her coldly. He had picked up her scent bottle and was holding it in the palm of his hand; almost absently Natalia watched it start to glow with growing brilliance. Kadir could make the glass shine with his purity of heart and his goodness? There must surely be some mistake.

'I will not allow you to foist this child off on me,' he repeated savagely, replacing the bottle on her dressing table before turning away from her.

Kadir could hardly bear to look at Natalia. So much indeed for those feelings, those hopes he had begun to allow himself to acknowledge he was experiencing, those cautious, vulnerable tendrils of the beginnings of a need within himself to forget the past and allow himself to believe that here on Niroli he could put aside the ghosts of his childhood and build a true future with Natalia and the children she would give him.

His own bitterness tasted sour on his tongue where so recently it had known the sweetness of Natalia's kiss. What sweetness? he challenged himself savagely. That so-called sweetness had masked acid-sharp poison. Did she really think he had become so vulnerable to her that she could openly foist another man's bastard on him without him challenging her? And running behind the violence of his justifiably angry thoughts was the pride-scouring knowledge that a part of him actually wished that she had not answered his question truthfully and that instead she had…that she had lied to him? Allowed him to believe that the child she carried was his?

Natalia waited until Kadir had left her to shut himself in his dressing room before daring to give way to her tears.

CHAPTER ELEVEN

SHE was not going to let them see how she felt, not now not ever, Natalia thought to herself as she watched the way Zahra clung to Kadir's arm as she laughed up flirtatiously at him.

Did anyone believe for one single minute that the other woman had really come to Niroli because she was interested in using some of the fortune left to her by her elderly late husband to finance a hotel and spa complex at a desert oasis some miles from the capital city of Hadiya, and thus wanted to know more about the success of Niroli's own resort? Or could they see right through what was so obviously a blatant plan on Kadir's part to bring his mistress to Niroli, even if publicly Zahra appeared to have arrived here under her own steam and on her own whim. To stay here permanently? Was it really only three months ago that the thought of her as-then-unmet husband having a mistress had been one she had accepted with calm equanimity? Natalia was forced to ask herself. How naïve she had been, and how very foolish.

King Giorgio was beckoning her over to join him. Forcing herself to smile as serenely as she could, Natalia made her way across the salon, dropping the king a deep formal curtsey before taking the seat he had waved her into.

'It is good that Kadir intends to maintain good relations with Hadiya. As two nations we have much to offer one another and much to learn from one another.'

'Prince Kadir is bound to feel a strong sense of allegiance towards the country of his birth, Your Highness,' Natalia responded calmly.

'That is indeed so, but Kadir's home is here now, our customs his customs. I understand you met Zahra Rafiq on your honeymoon visit to Hadiya—is that so?'

'Yes,' Natalia agreed woodenly.

To her astonishment the king reached for her hand and squeezed it gently. 'You are a good girl, Natalia, and I can see in your eyes and hear in your voice the pride you feel. That is only natural and right, of course, however—' the king paused '—over the course of my lifetime I have perhaps made more than my fair share of mistakes, errors of judgement that my pride would not allow me to admit at the time, but which I now bear on my conscience even though it is not my habit to admit as much to others. Kadir is a very proud man. How could he not be when he is my son? As Niroli's future King he will be all the things that I want him to be for Niroli, but even at my time of life, Natalia, there are surprises and unexpected discoveries. I had not thought, for instance, that I should love him so immediately and so very dearly. It is as though he has been a part of my heart from the beginning. It is through that love I bear him that I say to you now that I do not want him to suffer the unhappiness my own pride has sometimes caused me to suffer. I have seen the look in your eyes when you look at him when you think no one else is watching and I have seen too the way Kadir looks at you.'

Natalia could guess what the king was about to say.

'Sir, you need have no fear that either of us will let you down,' she assured him vehemently. 'We are both committed to our duty to Niroli. I…I cannot speak, of course, for Kadir's most private feelings but…' oh, how it tore at her heart to say that knowing those private feelings were given to Zahra '…but I know he will not allow them to come between him and that duty.'

Through his words, King Giorgio was making it clear that even he could see how much Kadir wished that he could have made Zahra his wife. It was more than Natalia could bear. Barely able to control her voice, she bowed her head and begged huskily, 'Sir, if I might have your permission to retire…'

'Your wife is leaving,' Zahra told Kadir with obvious triumph. She smiled up at him provocatively and stroked the sleeve of his jacket with her fingertips.

'Zahra, you should not have come here to Niroli,' Kadir told her wryly.

'How can you say that when I can see how much you need me?' she reproached him.

Kadir shook his head reprovingly. He had not been at all pleased when Zahra had presented herself at the palace claiming to officials that they were close friends, and insisting to him that all she wanted to do was to make use of the new trade opportunities opening up between the two countries. She'd said she'd wanted to remain his friend, but when he had taxed her with it Zahra had been so sweetly insistent that she fully understood that their relationship was over, whilst begging him not to be cruel to her and send her away, that Kadir had felt reluctantly compelled to allow her to stay, at least until her business negotiations were completed.

'I know now I should find someone else, Kadir,' she was telling him softly now. 'But how can I when you are the only man I want, and the only man I could ever want? I could never be your Queen, I know that now, but foolishly my heart can't help hoping that you might find a small place in your life for me, even if it is only that of a trusted and discreet friend with whom you can spend a few precious hours relaxing.'

'This is foolish talk, Zahra, and you know it.' Kadir had to stop her. 'I am a married man now with a country to rule and an example to set to my people.'

'But you need me, Kadir. We are destined to be together. We would be together if it wasn't for the meddling of your mother. It was only when that fool, your mother, revealed her lies to you that you put me to one side. Until then—'

'Enough! I will not hear you speak of my mother so. You forget that she was your Queen.' He was not going to let Zahra make him feel guilty about ending their relationship. He had hardly been her first lover, after all, and he'd always made the boundaries of their relationship clear. It had surprised him that his mother should have disliked her so intensely.

'Your mother betrayed her husband; she was not fit to be Queen.'

'That is enough!'

'She claimed the sheikh as your father when he was not,' Zahra continued ignoring him.

'You forget that she was little more than a child when she made the decision to conceal my conception from her husband.' What was he doing defending his mother, and, worse, echoing Natalia's passionate arguments to him? Kadir didn't know. All he did know was that Zahra's unexpectedly venomously angry criticism of his mother had filled him with a desire to protect his mother from her.

'Kadir, why are we quarrelling like this when we could be doing something so much more pleasurable?'

This was the Zahra Kadir knew, a wickedly provocative, wholly sensual woman, who knew very well how to please a man in bed.

But who left him cold emotionally?

Kadir shook both thoughts away. No matter what their relationship might have been in the past, there was no place here in his present or his future for it, and he had made that plain to Zahra from the moment he'd known he wanted to take up his father's offer to succeed him to the throne of Niroli.

'You should not have come here,' he repeated firmly. 'You must return to Hadiya; I think you already know that.'

She was looking away from him so that Kadir did not

see the flash of fury in her eyes as she bent her head and said submissively, 'Of course, as you wish, Kadir.'

It was unthinkable that Kadir should break with protocol here in the palace at this semi formal gathering of court officials and cause unwanted gossip by openly rejecting Zahra in front of everyone, but he still couldn't stop himself from removing her hand from his arm and stepping away from her.

Why had Natalia almost run from the room like that? He had seen her talking with the king. Had his father said something to her to upset her? Had he perhaps asked her when he might look forward to hearing the news he so longed to hear?

'You cannot deceive me, Kadir,' Zahra was saying. 'I know that it is me who you want. Let me be the one to give you your first child, not her, that nobody you have married. Let me give you your first son…come to me tonight and we can—'

'Zahra, you are talking nonsense and you know it,' Kadir checked her firmly. 'Besides, it's already too late,' he told her curtly. Natalia was already carrying a child she claimed was his, but which he knew quite simply could not be. After all, he had used a condom. It was far too convenient for her to suggest that the condom might have been flawed.

Like her? Like the feelings for her he did not want to admit to? He shook the thought of Natalia away and tried to focus on Zahra instead. What on earth had got into her? She knew it was out of the question that they should restart their relationship, never mind that she should have his child, and he couldn't understand why on earth she should be saying such nonsense. He hoped that letting her know that Natalia was already pregnant would underline those facts and bring her to her senses.

The door from their bedroom to Kadir's dressing room stood open, the space beyond it dark and empty. Wherever Kadir was he was not here in their private apartments. Wherever he was, Natalia taunted herself bitterly. It was three o' clock in the morning. Where else could he be other than in the bed of his mistress? No wonder he had been so adamant that Zahra should not stay at the palace, but should instead have the use of a small private villa close by for the duration of her visit. Her visit or her permanent residence?

To her shock the outer door to the bedroom suddenly opened. Through the shadows Natalia could see Kadir look across to the bed where she lay.

'What's wrong? Did you decide it might not be a good idea to spend the night with your mistress after all?'

Why had she said that? She had promised herself she would not humiliate herself by descending to that kind of revealing sarcasm, but, as Natalia was beginning to discover, her emotions were far stronger than her logic.

'And what exactly is that supposed to mean?'

Natalia could hear something beyond anger in Kadir's voice that could have been exhaustion, but she did not want to listen to it.

'You know exactly what I mean, Kadir. Zahra is your mistress; she made that plain enough to me in Hadiya. You invited her to come here and tonight you made it plain to everyone just what your relationship with her is.'

'I did not send for Zahra.' He had dropped down onto his own side of the bed and was sitting there with his back to her, Natalia saw as she switched on her own bedside light.

'You don't really expect me to believe that, do you?' she threw at him scornfully.

'Yes, as a matter of fact I do,' he told her angrily. 'You see, unlike you I do not lie and use deceit.'

'Unlike me! You criticise me as freely as though you know everything there is to know about me, Kadir. And yet the truth is you know nothing about me, because if you did you would know that whilst, yes, I understand and enjoy my sexuality—what woman of my age does not unless she has serious issues on both counts—but that does not mean that I abuse it. In fact it may interest you to know that prior to my folly in Venice in giving in to…to what we did, I had been celibate for well over five years—and by choice. You, of course, will not believe that because you would much rather believe the worst you can of me because that reinforces your decision to think badly of your mother and you have to do that otherwise you might— just might,' she told him bitterly, 'find yourself having to admit that you misjudged her. And that would mean that she died longing for your forgiveness and being refused it—'

'No…'

His tormented denial shamed her back to reality. No matter how unhappy she was, that did not give her the right to try to hurt him, and, besides, the truth was that in reality she loved him too much to want to do so.

Loved him! How that knowledge tore at her vulnerable heart, and how she wished it were not so.

A terse apology quivered on the tip of her tongue but before she could offer it he repeated, 'No...you are wrong. I did...that is... No matter what I thought privately I could not let her die thinking... Of course I told her that I understood. How could I not? She was my mother...'

There was a huge lump in Natalia's throat. 'I'm... I'm sorry,' she told him huskily. 'I should not have said that.'

'No, you shouldn't have,' Kadir agreed tiredly. 'And as for your accusation that Zahra is my mistress. Yes, once that was true, but it ceased to be true with my mother's death. Zahra's decision to come here had nothing to do with me and I have made it clear to her that there is no place here for her, and certainly not in my life or my bed.'

Could that be true, and, if it were, perhaps this sudden mood of admittedly somewhat hostile exchange of confidences between them could lead to a better understanding between them? Perhaps that might mean that in time... What? That in time he would love her?

'So if you haven't been with her, then where have you been?' she challenged him.

'Driving...and then walking.' Abruptly he changed the subject. 'You say you were celibate before Venice. I am not a fool, Natalia. I've seen just what a woman will do to protect the child she carries. My mother told me that it was not out of love for King Giorgio that she allowed her husband to believe he was my father, it was out of love for me, her child. She told me that when a woman conceives a child, no matter what her feelings or her moral stance was before, from the moment she knows of the new life she carries within her, protecting that life becomes her prime concern. In many ways you remind me of my mother. You share the same concern for others and the same strength of purpose and spirit.'

'And because of that you believe that I would lie to you about the paternity of your child—is that what you are saying?' Natalia asked him.

It seemed incredible that they should be having a conversation of such intimacy when less than an hour ago she had believed him to be holding another woman in his arms. How odd and unfair it was that she should be able to accept his words as the truth when he could not do the same with hers. But then she did not have his experience with his mother to contend with.

'You are lying to me. I know that.'

'That is not true. I am telling you the truth. This baby is your baby.'

'Perhaps I shouldn't have told you I was pregnant,' Natalia burst out miserably when he made no response. 'Perhaps I should have held back the truth and let you think I had conceived after we were married,' she told him. 'Only, you see, I didn't want to think that the future relationship I hoped we might have together had been built on a lie.' She put her hand on her stomach. 'This *is* your child, Kadir. If you can't believe that—or me—then there are always DNA tests,' she reminded him, hating herself for being so weak as to offer him this instead of insisting that he accept her word. 'Although they cannot be done until after the baby is born.'

'Do you think I'm completely stupid? We used protection—this child cannot be mine and so there is only one way the situation can be resolved.'

'And that is?' Natalia demanded shakily.

'A document must be drawn up which you will sign stating that this child is not mine and therefore cannot be my heir nor ascend to the throne of Niroli on my death.'

Natalia stared at his unbowed back. 'I don't understand what you are saying,' she told him, but she was horribly, sickeningly afraid that she did. 'Do you really expect me to sign away my child—our child's rights to its paternity? Do you really think I would do that to our baby?'

'Your baby,' Kadir corrected her coldly. 'This child is none of my doing, Natalia, and I will never accept it as such. So either you agree to sign such a document or I will have to go to King Giorgio and tell him that the marriage will have to be put aside and why.'

'You can't do that,' Natalia whispered.

How could she tell him after what he had just said that she had truly come to believe that, somehow or other, illogical and fantastical though it seemed, something deep within her *had* somehow recognised in Venice all that he would come to mean to her, and that as a result fate had willed that she would conceive his child.

'I don't want to,' he surprised her by admitting. 'I have my father's feelings to think of. He personally chose you to be my wife. He is a very proud man, and to learn what you are would humiliate him. Plus, your lack of sexual morals aside, rather surprisingly in the short time in which we have been married I have come to recognise how well equipped in other ways you are to be Niroli's Queen, and how much the island will benefit from having you as their Queen,' he told her sombrely. 'Together we can work to give this island and its people all that they deserve to have, but I cannot and will not allow this bastard child to claim me as its father. You will do well to keep the child out of my way because it will for ever remind me of all the reasons why I have learned to doubt and mistrust your sex.'

Kadir thought about the hours he had just spent battling with himself, with what he truly believed was right. He had forced himself to admit how much she had already come to mean to him, and how much he wanted her by his side, but he could not overcome his fury that she continued to try to force on him a child he knew could not be his.

'The choice is yours,' he told her as he got up off the bed.

'And if I refuse?' Natalia asked him, dry-mouthed. But of course she already knew the answer. 'Kadir, please, this is your own child you are talking about,' she begged him. 'The condom must have perished. The baby can have DNA tests and I promise you this is your child. You can monitor them yourself. Kadir, you grew up with a father who turned his back on you. You know how much that hurts and the pain it causes a child.'

'Don't ask me to lie to you, Natalia, because I won't. I'm afraid I can't see how this can be my child. I will sleep in my dressing room tonight.'

Natalia lay back against her pillows after he had gone.

He was offering her so much that she wanted, but at such a dreadful price. She could not and would not allow him to deny their child its right to his or her true paternity, but she could not force him to give the baby his love any more than she could force him to give it to her. Why, why, why had this had to happen? If only she had not gone to Venice, if only she had not met him until their wedding day… But why say that, why not ask herself why Kadir could not accept her word, why could he not accept the gift of herself she had already given him and the gift of his child that came from that night? But she knew the answer to that, didn't she? Kadir's inability to trust the female sex was very deeply rooted indeed.

Well, she would not let him punish their child because of what he himself had suffered in his own childhood. If he rejected it, then she would find a way of providing it with loving male influences from within her own family. She would protect and love their baby no matter what Kadir said, and even if it meant closing the door for ever on the love she had so longed to see grow between them.

CHAPTER TWELVE

NIROLI was experiencing one of its fortunately rare periods of bad weather, with fierce winds lashing the coast and whipping up the waves; grey skies had replaced the normal sunny blue and the outlook from the window of the salon in their private apartments looked dauntingly bleak. But nowhere near as bleak as her own future and the future of the child she was carrying, Natalia acknowledged.

She had planned to spend the morning working on her notes for a series of talks she'd been invited to give to Niroli's young women, the mothers to be of the next generation. She had planned to talk to them of the many opportunities she hoped would be available, not just for their unborn children, but for them, as well, but now the words of hope and encouragement and excitement simply would not flow. All she could think of was the poor child growing within her body and the fact that it would not have the opportunity to be loved by its father, the opportunity to grow up confidently and happily in a loving atmosphere, secure in its knowledge of its place in the world. Maybe these were the issues she should be addressing in her speech; the sadness of children born without love, unwanted, their chances of human fulfilment in all its most important senses pitifully crushed before they even drew breath. What did her vision of a new wonderful Niroli have to offer these children? Natalia pushed back the laptop on which she had been working and stood up. Today, because there'd been no formal engagements, unlike Kadir who was due to go on a tour of the island's vineyards, she had dressed in her own clothes, a soft off-white fine wool long sleeved top worn loosely beneath a tunic top in pale grey, worn over a gently flowing black shirt. It was one of her favourite outfits, designed by a talented young local designer. It was one of Natalia's dreams to be able to establish the kind of art college on Niroli that ultimately would attract tutors and students from all over the world.

She heard the door to the salon opening and turned round to see who it was, her heart sinking when she saw Zahra closing the door and standing between her and it.

The last person she felt like being with right now was her husband's mistress; her husband's ex-mistress, she corrected herself.

Kadir had after all sworn that that was the truth, and if she expected him to accept her own words as the truth then she could do no less for him.

'Is it true that you are to have Kadir's child?' Zahra demanded without preamble.

Her bluntness took Natalia slightly aback, but more importantly and more hurtfully was the knowledge that the only way Zahra could know about her pregnancy was because Kadir had told her about it himself. So much then for there not being any intimacy between Kadir and Zahra. After all, it was hardly the kind of information one would just throw into a conversation with one's supposedly ex-mistress, was it?

And when had he told her? Last night after she had finally drifted into an exhausted and unhappy sleep? Had he gone then to his mistress seeking solace with her because of his feelings about their child?

'Is it?' Zahra pressed her.

There was an almost fevered look about her, Natalia noticed uncasily, a wildness about her eyes and her manner, her movements uncoordinated and slightly jerky as though she was not fully in control of herself.

'Whether or not I am to have a child is surely a private matter,' Natalia answered with quiet dignity.

Zahra ignored her attempt to apply discretion to the situation by telling her passionately, 'Kadir has no secrets from me. He tells me everything. Everything,' she repeated fiercely. 'Do you understand? I know you are to have his child, but of course he doesn't want it. How could he?'

Natalia felt a wave of sickness surge through her, draining her strength. Until she had heard those last few telling words she had tried to convince herself that Zahra was exaggerating the extent of the intimacy she shared with Kadir, but now with that damning 'he does not want it' she was forced to accept the truth. Kadir had called *her* a liar, but he was the one who was obviously lying. No, she could not bear to go there. She must not let Zahra see how much she had upset her; she must think of her child instead.

'You say nothing, but I know it is true. Your very silence gives you away,' she could hear Zahra raging. 'You think you've won, don't you?' she told Natalia furiously. 'You think that just because Kadir has impregnated you he is yours, but he is not and he never will be. You may have conceived but you have yet to give birth. A king needs sons, heirs, live children…and you will never bear those.'

Something was going dreadfully wrong. She could sense it, taste and smell it almost in the air that separated her from Zahra. The other woman's words now surely had turned away from those of a jealous, vengeful mistress determined to stake her claim in a shared man and had instead become a direct threat to Natalia herself. The first tiny tendrils of fear began to unfurl coldly inside Natalia's stomach.

Where were her maids and the countess? It was too late now to regret insisting that she preferred to be left alone unless she sent for them. Zahra was standing between her and the main doors into the public corridor. The other doors in the room, which were further away, led towards the rest of the apartment, which was empty.

Surely, though, she was being overly dramatic, something that perhaps all newly pregnant women were inclined to be when it came to the safety of their unborn child, Natalia reasoned, but no sooner had she offered herself the comfort of this thought, Zahra began to rant.

'Do you really think I will let you take Kadir from me? Do you really think that just because you tell him that you are to have a child that he will choose you above me? If so you are a fool. Because he won't. I won't let that happen. Not ever. I am the one he loves and wants. I am the one who is destined to stand by his side. Kadir is mine. Our sons will be his male heirs, and not yours. He can never be yours.'

Suddenly the tone of Zahra's voice had dropped to a chilling hiss that brought up the hairs at the back of Natalia's neck in warning.

'I will kill you first! You and your child. I will slit your throat and then tear the child you carry from your belly before I let you take Kadir from me.'

Zahra was mad. Completely and totally insane, Natalia recognised in a rush of shocked horror. Insane and dangerous, she admitted, icy cold fear gripping her as Zahra's words sank in. Instinctively Natalia looked towards the door. Quick as lightning Zahra intercepted and correctly interpreted her look.

'It is no use. You cannot escape.'

She must do something to try to calm her down, Natalia recognised. She must not panic and make an already dangerous situation even worse by playing into Zahra's hands. Someone would come, they were bound to do so. Desperately she tried to force herself to think past her panic and her instinctive and urgent need to protect her baby, to use logic, calming measures to diffuse the situation.

'There's no need for this, Zahra,' she told her, trying to keep her voice calm and steady. 'I don't want to take Kadir from you.' If she could just skirt round Zahra and get to the inner corridor doors she could escape into the corridor and lock herself in her bedroom until she could summon help.

'You're lying. You love him and you want him for yourself. I have seen it in your eyes. You have told him that you are carrying his child in an attempt to keep him, but it will not work, because you will not be carrying it for much longer.'

To Natalia's horror Zahra suddenly reached within the flowing sleeve of the long gown she was wearing and produced a wickedly sharp-looking curved and pointed dagger.

There was no doubt now that Zahra *was* totally insane, Natalia recognised numbly. There was no point in her trying to reason with her because wherever Zahra was it was somewhere way beyond listening to any kind of logical reasoning.

'First it was that mother of his who stopped him from marrying me,' she panted as she started to move towards Natalia. 'She did not approve of me. She did not think I was good enough for Kadir. And now because of her and her lies there is you, a European nobody who Kadir has been forced to marry. But he doesn't want you. He wants me. And I want him. Only you stand between us and our happiness. It is my duty to kill you, because it is my duty to make Kadir happy, and I am the only one who can give him true happiness.'

She had to reach those inner doors, Natalia knew, because if she didn't Zahra would try to harm her baby and try to kill her. She was the taller of the two of them and the more athletic, but she had no knowledge of how to use a knife or how to defend herself from one and from the slashing stabbing movements Zahra was making as she stalked her. Zahra was well versed in handling the murderous-looking weapon she was holding.

Even if she turned and ran for the doors, they were heavy and not easy to open and Zahra would be on her before she could do so, bringing that dagger down to rip and tear at her flesh.

Oh, what was she to do? Natalia found that she was praying silently for strength and help, begging God or anyone who was nearby to please help her and, more importantly, her baby.

The vines were in their resting period, row upon row of immaculately tended brown stems. As he watched and listened to Giovanni Carini, Natalia's grandfather, as he lovingly described their virtues and their vices to him it was as though he were talking about his children, Kadir recognised. Each vine was known to him and cherished for its individuality.

'And these are the new vines that were the gift to us of Rosa Fierezza,' Giovanni told him proudly. 'Their strength grafted onto our own vines will produce our best wines yet.'

'You obviously love them as though they were Nirolian born,' Kadir teased him gently.

'Surely it is every man's duty to cherish that which is a gift of love as much if not more than that which he has created himself?' Gioivanni told him steadfastly.

Suddenly, out of nowhere, inside his head Kadir could see an image of his mother as she had been in her last weeks, frail in body but the strength of her spirit shining through as she begged him to be proud of his true paternity.

'Niroli will benefit from all that you bring to ruling it, Kadir, just as Hadiya would have done had you chosen to take up your inheritance there. Your brother is a good administrator, and a fair and kind man, but you are the one who has the vision and the passion that is needed by a true leader and those are your gifts from your natural father. I beg you, do not turn aside from them or scorn them.'

His mother… How she would have loved Natalia. And the child Natalia was carrying? As clearly as though she had been standing at his side he could hear his mother's voice telling him softly, 'Do not deny your child, Kadir; do not turn away this precious gift, out of fear.'

Was *that* it? Was his refusal to accept that he was the father of the child Natalia was carrying based on fear? He knew perfectly well, despite having denied it to Natalia, that condoms were not always reliable; what man did not? In every other way Natalia had proved to him over and over again her honesty and her strong moral code through the things she said and did. Was it therefore so very unlikely that she would not tell him the truth about this child…? This child… His child. And he wanted to believe her, didn't he? He wanted her to be truly his wife, his partner, his, totally and completely. Again he felt that sharp stab of fear. The fear of a man deeply in love so lacking in true strength that he feared he was not able to win and hold the love of the woman he loved so deeply, because in the past he had felt unloved?

Kadir had never imagined that he would ever be called upon to look so deeply within himself and question his own motivations. But when a man fell deeply in love, the way he looked at everything changed.

Deeply in love? Him? With Natalia? Well, wasn't he? Wasn't that what this was all about? Was he really not man enough to accept her word that this child was his? What if their positions were reversed? What if he was being accused of having fathered a child who was not his, for instance, and she refused to believe him? How would he feel? All at once Kadir knew he needed to see Natalia and talk to her, honestly and openly, to lay before her his own insecurities and his love for her. He had been the first man, the only man she had slept with in many years, she had told him. How did accepting the truth of that admission make him feel? Didn't it make him ache to wrap his arms around her and tell her just what it did to him to know that her immediate and overwhelming desire for him had led her to break her own rules and show him how she felt? He looked discreetly at his watch. The tour was only half over, it would be several hours yet before he could return to the palace.

A sudden powerful surge of wind bent the vines to the ground, whistling as it ripped through the air around them, followed by the splatter of heavy rain.

'It is the notorious Niroli storm,' Giovanni told them. 'They come out of nowhere from the sea, blessedly infrequently, but when they do come...' He was looking anxiously at his precious vines and Kadir could see that he was impatient to do what he could to protect them.

'Your Highness, we should perhaps head back to the palace,' one of his aides was suggesting, 'at least until the storm blows over.' He was having to raise his voice so that Kadir could hear him above the increasing howl of the gale now battering them.

Kadir nodded his head, thinking ruefully that, whilst he wished the vines of Niroli no harm, he couldn't help but be pleased that the storm was giving him an excuse to be with Natalia.

Natalia! The urgency of his desire to be with her was pounding inside his head and his heart, driving him, and for once in his life he was determined to follow his instincts and his heart and not his head and logic.

The first person Kadir saw as he walked into the palace was the countess.

'My wife?' he asked her. 'Is she…?'

'She is in your apartments, Your Highness. She asked not to be disturbed, but if you wish me to tell her that you—'

'No, there is no need, I will go myself,' Kadir said, thanking her.

'You cannot escape, you know that, don't you?' Zahra told Natalia. 'Even if you scream and someone hears you, by the time they get here it will be far too late.'

Natalia was struggling to accept what was happening. She knew that inwardly she had likened the previous intensity of Zahra's manner to that of a potential stalker, and she had, too, felt irritated by Kadir's typical male inability to see beyond the adoring, soft-as-butter, man-pleasing façade Zahra put up whenever she saw him, but it had never occurred to her that Zahra might physically attack her. The very idea seemed outlandish and like something out of a bad film. But it wasn't a film and it was happening to her.

'Zahra, you need to think about this and about what your own future will be if you go ahead,' Natalia urged her, striving desperately to bring down the tension by talking matter of factly about what was happening. 'You won't be able to escape. You will go to prison and how can you be with Kadir then?'

Zahra, though, was refusing to be sidetracked. 'Kadir will protect me,' she insisted. 'He is beyond the law and so I will be, too. Besides, why would anyone mourn you? You are nothing…and once I have given Kadir his first son no one will remember that you ever existed, but first of course I have to destroy the child you are carrying and you with it.'

How could she sound so casual? Surely only some kind of mental disorder could be responsible for such behaviour? And that surely meant that there was no point in trying to reason with Zahra. She had to try to get to those doors, Natalia recognised. There was no other chance of escape from her. With every deadly word Zahra uttered her madness became more clear. There was no point in trying to reason with her.

Natalia tried to judge the distance she would have to run; if she feinted and pretended to make for the far set of doors that might draw Zahra off and allow her to get behind her to the main set.

She took a deep breath and said a small prayer to her

guardian angel, if she had one, and to her child for its forgiveness if they didn't make it.

She must focus on the doors, on getting them open and getting out. Abruptly the main door to the suite opened, causing both women to turn towards them.

'Kadir…' Natalia sobbed his name in sick relief as she saw her husband standing there. Whilst he might have encouraged Zahra to come here to be with him, Natalia did not believe for one minute that he could have known of her obviously hidden precarious mental state.

'What the—?'

Kadir took in the scene with one brief glance around the room. 'Zahra,' he began but she didn't let him continue.

Without taking her eyes off Natalia, she said with mad glee, 'It is all right, Kadir. Soon she will not come between us any more because I shall have killed her and the brat she carries.'

'Guards. *Guards!*' Kadir called out urgently into the corridor as Zahra made a swift lunge towards Natalia, ripping the sleeve of Natalia's top with the downward plunge of her dagger as Natalia dodged her and started to run for the now-open doors. Natalia was fast, but Zahra's madness had obviously given her even greater speed. Natalia could hear the sound of her breathing behind her, she felt the sharp, biting sting of the blade as it sliced into the flesh of her shoulder and then, incredibly, unbelievably and surely impossibly, just as she thought there would be no escape for her after all, Kadir, who must have moved at the speed of light, threw himself protectively in between them to shield her and to take the full force of Zahra's savage stab towards his heart.

The last thing Natalia heard before she fainted was the soft, low grunt of pain Kadir gave as he fell forwards onto her.

'Your Highness, the woman Zahra Rafiq was intercepted on her way to the airport. She has refused to undergo a medical examination here in Niroli. We have therefore as you instructed been in contact with the necessary authorities in Hadiya and they have given permission for her to be escorted there to undergo a medical assessment and receive treatment.'

Kadir's mouth compressed. He knew he would never cease to blame himself for not realising the dark truth Zahra had been concealing behind her mask of apparent sanity. Natalia, saint that she was, might have urged him to think compassionately of her and to understand that her behaviour sprang from an undiagnosed mental condition, but for the moment Kadir was finding that hard to do. The true guilt, of course, was his own for not realising the truth about Zahra himself, and he doubted he would ever forgive himself for that.

Having thanked the minister for his report he turned to the palace aide waiting anxiously to talk with him. 'King Giorgio is most anxious to see you, Highness,' he told Kadir. 'The news of the dreadful attack on you and the Crown Princess could not be kept from him and he is beside himself with anxiety.'

'Please tell my father that I am well and that I shall

be with him as soon as I have spoken with the Crown Princess's consultant.'

Not even to reassure his father did Kadir intend to leave the hospital until he had spoken with Natalia and told her what he had to say.

He knew that from now until his dying day he would never, ever forget the emotions that that seized him when he had thrust open the doors to the apartment and seen what had been happening. The reality of her own imminent death had already been shadowing Natalia's eyes, her hands clasped across her body to protect her, *his* child, and in that moment all he had known, his single and only thought, had been his need to protect them both. Not just Natalia, but the child she carried as well, for he had known instinctively then, when it was almost too late, that the baby could not have been fathered by anyone other than himself. He had felt protective of the baby and he'd been filled with the most tender love for him or her. Who would protect them both if he did not do so, who had more responsibility, more right to stand between them and whatever harm might threaten them? His wife… His child…

His last thought as he had begun to lose consciousness had been that he loved them both almost beyond bearing.

It had therefore been a shock to arrive at the hospital, still barely conscious himself from his loss of blood, to be told there was a grave danger that Natalia might lose the baby—all the more so because of his own only just discovered feelings. 'You must save the baby,' he had told them as they had worked to cleanse his wound—not, fortunately, as deep as it had first looked and not having damaged any vital organs despite the flow of blood.

'We will do our best,' they had assured him, not knowing his concern was not because the child was his heir, but because he knew how distraught Natalia would be if she were to lose it, and how he couldn't bear it if neither she nor the baby ever got to know how wrong he had been and how much he loved them both.

In her hospital bed, Natalia stared anxiously up at the consultant.

'My husband—how is he?' she asked him, realising even now when she was still in shock that, as Niroli's Crown Prince, Kadir's safety was paramount for his people and she surely must remember that.

'The Crown Prince is fine apart from a small flesh wound,' the consultant assured her. 'He is waiting outside to see you now.'

Natalia nodded her head, and then looked at him. 'You are sure...about...about the baby?' she pleaded with him, tears filling her eyes. They had already removed the drip they had used to replace fluids and she'd also been mildly sedated to keep her calm whilst they fought to prevent her from losing her child. 'There's no mistake...?' she begged him.

'No, there is no mistake,' the consultant confirmed tiredly. It had been a long night and they had been anxious to save the Crown Prince, the Princess and their baby.

The door to her room was opening. The consultant gave Kadir a small bow, before leaving them alone together.

'Thank you for…for saving my life.'

Kadir grimaced. He looked tired and drained. The blood-soaked shirt he'd been wearing had been replaced by a clean one; the wound Zahra had inflicted was now cleaned and dressed.

'If I saved you, then it was only right that I should have done so since I was the one who put you both at risk in the first place. I had no idea about Zahra…she never showed any signs… When I told her that there was no point in her trying to remain here on Niroli, and reinforced that by reminding her that you are my wife and that you were to have a child, I never imagined for one moment…'

Something in the obvious sincerity of his shocked and earnest demeanour broke through Natalia's protective distance. She wanted to reach out and touch him, tell him, but how could she now when she knew what he must be thinking about the baby? He probably would have wanted her to lose it, even if he was not prepared to admit as much to her. She knew that. How could she not after the way he had refused to accept that the baby was his? 'You weren't to know. I expect she wasn't even aware that she was suffering from a mental illness herself. It's sad really…poor woman…' Natalia told him emotionlessly. 'But there's no reason for you to blame yourself.'

'On the contrary, there is every reason. You are my wife, it is my duty to protect you, I should have realised…'

'Have they told you yet about…about the baby?' Natalia asked him in a low voice.

Kadir nodded his head.

'I expect you think that it would also have been for the best if I had lost it, as they feared I would.'

She could not bring herself to look at him. Throughout the long hours when she had lain sedated whilst her baby had fought so hard to hold onto life she had known that Kadir must have been hoping equally hard that it would not. That hurt her far more than anything that Zahra had done to her.

'Natalia…'

The door to her room opened and an aide stood there. 'Your Highness,' he began, obviously flustered. 'The king…King Giorgio is here. He will not accept that you are alive and well until he has seen you for himself…'

The king was here? The king who never left his palace and who expected others always to dance to his will? Natalia's eyes widened. She had seen for herself the way in which his love for Kadir had softened the king's arrogance and warmed his heart, but this was evidence indeed of how much Kadir had come to mean to him.

'You must go to him,' she told Kadir quickly, reminding him, 'He is an old man, Kadir, and he must have been badly frightened.'

Kadir inclined his head. 'Very well,' he told her, 'but I shall return as soon as I can.'

No sooner had Kadir gone than the consultant returned carrying an envelope.

'These are copies of the scans we did of the baby,' he told her with a small smile. 'As you know, we do not advocate the use of our wonderful new scanner merely as a means of detecting a child's sex before its birth so that the parents can know what colour to decorate the nursery, but, since we had to do these scans to check that the baby was okay, I wondered if you might wish to have them?'

Smiling through the sudden emotion of her tears, Natalia took them from him.

'I did ask the Crown Prince if he would like to see them but he refused…'

'Yes,' Natalia agreed quietly. 'He would.'

'He said that you should be the first to see them,' the consultant told her, oblivious to the true meaning of her quiet and very sad words. 'You might not want to see them if you don't want to find out the sex of the baby— it is quite clear from these images.'

'No, that's okay, I'd love to know.'

'But, either way, it is good to know that the future King of Niroli values a daughter as much as a son. When I offered him the chance to discover the sex of the child you are carrying he said that its sex did not matter, only that it should live.'

Natalia stiffened in disbelief. 'I can't imagine…that is…he didn't really want…'

As though he had guessed some of what she was feeling and could not say, the consultant told her gently, 'The whole of Niroli knows that your marriage is a matter of state, but no one seeing the Crown Prince with you during these last worrying hours could doubt that, whatever might have been, he is now a man very much in love with and devoted to his wife. You were his first concern when you were all brought here. He begged us to attend to you first and he has remained here outside your room throughout the night. In fact at one time my nurse was forced to report to me that he had disobeyed my instructions and that she had found him sitting here with you watching over you whilst you were unconscious. Now, please promise me that you will accept that you need have no more fears for the safety of your baby. I do assure you that all is well and the crisis safely past.'

Natalia nodded her head. Kadir had said that to the consultant? He couldn't have meant it though—could he? She stifled a sleepy yawn. The consultant had warned her that she would feel tired for several days after all that she had been through and that her body would compel her to sleep to give both her and her baby a chance to recuperate fully. She looked at the envelope the consultant had left for her and then opened it slowly, studying the three-dimensional images inside it, her tears blurring her gaze as she saw her beautiful baby looking back at her. The baby she could so easily have lost...the baby she could so easily never have conceived in the first place.

Natalia was asleep when Kadir returned to her room and settled himself on the chair beside her bed. He looked down at the smooth bedclothes covering her still-flat body. His father's emotions as he had held him and reassured himself that he was truly alive had touched a well spring of responsive emotion within himself. He reached out and placed his hand on Natalia's body. He didn't need to struggle to recall how he had felt during the long hours of the night fearing with every heartbeat that she might lose the child she was carrying. That memory would remain with him for ever.

'I have prayed for you, little one,' he murmured

softly, 'and my prayers have been answered. Be assured that you shall have my love for always and that I shall be a true father to you, just as you are already a true son to me, the son of my heart, as well as of my body, loved and held in my heart for always. You and your mother shall have the greatest gift I can give you and that is the gift of my love for the whole of your lives.'

'*Kadir.*' Natalia's voice was thick with tears. She had heard him come in but she had not opened her eyes, not realising that he would think she was still asleep.

'I mean it,' he told her, reaching out for her hand and clasping it between his own. 'I do mean it, Natalia. I love you. *You*, Natalia Carini, you, the bold, exciting woman who showed me her pride in her sexuality and shamed my own foolish blindness to the real reason I fought so hard against my love for you. Fear is a terrible thing, all the more so when that fear belongs to a man who refuses to accept that he can feel it, and gives it other names instead. Natalia, my wife, my love, my life, you are my love, even if I have refused until now to fully recognise that love.' He took a deep raw breath of air. 'When I saw Zahra with that knife and realised what she was going to do, it wasn't just your life I knew I had to protect, it was the child's, as well. You need have no fear that this child, this son, who I now freely accept as being my own child, will not suffer as I did. He *shall* be my son and I shall be his father, my first-born son, I love him as that already.'

'Your son?' Natalia asked him softly. She could barely keep the smile back from her lips or out of her voice. Her happiness was welling up inside her like champagne bubbles.

'Well, I don't want to disappoint you, Kadir, but actually this son you plan to love is going to be a daughter…' Still smiling, she handed him the scan pictures.

She might know now that Kadir was prepared to accept that their child was his, but somehow she knew that Kadir would fall totally and besottedly in love with his daughter in a way he would not have done with a son. Later, fate willing she would present him and the people of Niroli with a male heir, but for now to know she carried this precious wonderful gift of a daughter was almost more happiness than she could bear.

'A daughter…' Kadir marvelled as he looked at the images, his eyes bright with emotion.

'I thought we might name her for your mother…' Natalia suggested hesitantly. 'I…I thought about her when I was afraid and alone with Zahra and I prayed…'

Kadir's hand covered hers. 'I, too,' he told her thickly. Silently they looked at one another and then Kadir leaned towards her. 'Oh, my love, my dearest, dearest love. If I should have lost you.'

'But you didn't and you won't,' Natalia assured him as she lifted her face for his kiss.

A nurse coming to check on Natalia opened the door and then quickly withdrew. Who would have thought that a royal couple could behave like that—just like everyone else, holding one another and kissing so passionately that they were oblivious to her unwitting interruption?

* * *

'You know, I really think that she does have a look of my mother,' Kadir told Natalia judiciously later as they studied the scans together for the umpteenth time.

'No, she definitely has your nose,' Natalia corrected him firmly.

EPILOGUE

'THE Fierezza genes are astonishingly vigorous,' Natalia heard Emily Fierezza, the wife of Prince Marco, saying laughingly to the women of the family gathered in the courtyard. They were preparing to leave for the cathedral where Kadir was to be formally crowned and anointed as Niroli's new King.

'I've lost count of how many new babies have arrived or are about to arrive. You will tell me if you start feeling tired, won't you?' Emily pressed Natalia. 'Only Kadir made me swear that I would watch over you like a hawk.'

'You and the countess and pretty much the rest of the royal household.' Natalia laughed as she waited to enter her carriage, one of several that would form the coronation procession that would escort Kadir to the cathedral as Niroli's Crown Prince and then back again as its new King.

'I can't get over the change in King Giorgio. I never thought I'd see him looking so happy and relaxed. Marco says it's like discovering a grandfather he never knew he had, and it's all thanks to you and Kadir. Marco says that, between you, you've humanised him.'

'I haven't done anything,' Natalia protested. 'I think it's more that King Giorgio has come to realise how important a loving family is and that one has to give love in order to receive it.'

'Kadir will make Niroli a wonderful King, Natalia,' Emily told her warmly. 'We all think so.'

Tears pricked at Natalia's eyes. 'You know how much it means to Kadir to have so much family support.'

'He and Marco have such a lot in common. They are both very determined and independent, true Fierezza men.'

They certainly were, and her own Fierezza man had that extra something very special that came to him via his mother's blood, Natalia acknowledged. A small secret smile curled the corners of her mouth, her gaze hazing with sensual memories. Initially Kadir had insisted on reining in his passionate desire for her because of their baby, but last night he had been swept away by her on the full tide of her own longing for him, and her assurances that it was perfectly safe. He had loved her with tenderness and intimate sensuality, in such a way that her body still ached a little from their shared pleasure. Her skin still remembered the heat of the kisses he had lavished on it, every sensitive place visited and then revisited until she had not been able to stop herself from crying out to him in hot, sweet arousal. He was so very much a man. Her man, and, as she had whispered to him last night as she had re-voyaged over that territory she had explored the first time she had touched him, she truly did believe that something in her at some deep, little understood level had recognised him as her soul mate.

'Once I would not have believed you,' he told her in turn. 'But now, how can I deny it when every breath I take is witness to my love for you? I am so very blessed, Natalia,' he told her as he kissed her throat and then her jaw, his deliberate slowness making her ache for the feel of his mouth on her own. 'I have you, and our child…a father who loves me, a country that, with you at my side to guide me, has taken me into their hearts. Truly I am indeed blessed.'

And then he kissed her and Natalia knew that nothing in the world could possibly ever mean more to her than this man and the child he had given her. Just thinking about last night was making her body ache with longing for Kadir. But now that ache was edged with the delicious eroticism of anticipation instead of the pain of doubt. Tonight she would hold him and touch him and show him…

'Princess, it is time,' the countess announced importantly, bringing her out of her secret sensual daydream by gesturing to the waiting maids to pick up the train of Natalia's coronation gown.

There had not been such an occasion in the whole lifetime of many of the people gathered in the square and along the streets, lining the way to the cathedral, and Natalia could hear their cheers of encouragement and delight as the old fashioned horse-drawn coaches bowled past them.

She would merely be an observer at this, the formal

handing-over of the crown by King Giorgio to Kadir, but later she and Kadir planned to renew their vows to one another, in front of their people.

The cathedral was packed, its lofty spires reaching up into the bright blue sky, the hum of excited voices filling its cavernous interior.

But there was still, too, that quiet sense of spirit and belief; that awareness of times past and vows made, Natalia recognised as she joined the procession entering the cathedral.

At its head was King Giorgio escorting Kadir, but they were too far away for Natalia to be able to see Kadir's face, even though she could see the royal-blue velvet of his ceremonial cloak and the dark sheen of his bared head.

The sound of choir voices filled the air, rising on it like the most perfect notes of the most perfect scent. Today Kadir was wearing her special gift to him, a cologne she had made for him combining the most rare and special of ingredients to reflect the depths of her love for him and the beyond-price gift that he was giving to the people of Niroli in committing himself to them.

The king and Kadir had reached the two thrones waiting for them.

Natalia joined the other close members of the family in their designated pews.

The Archbishop of Niroli began the service of dedication. The ebb and flow of the solemn words of the ritual filled the ancient building, the reverence and awe of what was happening reflected in the radiance shining from the faces of the people as they said a respectful farewell to the king who had served them for so long and then turned with hope and confidence to the son who would, with his blessing, take his place.

'May you be blessed with many years in which to enjoy the fruits of your labours, King Giorgio,' the Archbishop prayed.

'And no doubt many years to interfere in the lives of the fruits of his loins,' Emily whispered ruefully to Natalia with fond affection.

They had grown especially close since it was the generosity of Marco, Emily's husband, and the worrisome health at one stage of their own now perfectly healthy child, that had led them to give the scanner to Niroli's maternity wing.

'He has grown very tired these last months,' Natalia whispered back, 'and, although he is far too proud to admit it, I think he would have been in despair if he still hadn't found an heir.'

They both fell silent as the choir stopped singing and King Giorgio rose from his throne to take the crown and place it on Kadir's head.

A hush filled the cathedral as though everyone there held their breath, and not just those inside the cathedral, but those outside in the square who were watching the ceremony on the giant TV screens that had been erected there.

The old king's hands trembled visibly but the crown held fast. There was a collective release of breath as the archbishop began the prayer of ordination and then asked Kadir the three requisite times if he accepted the Crown of Niroli.

His final firm assent had barely died away when the old king clasped Kadir's shoulders and spoke emotionally as though unable to hold back the words.

'My son.'

Natalia suspected she wasn't the only one with tears in her eyes when Kadir replied equally informally and emotionally, 'My father.' When they embraced the roar of approval from the crowd rolled in from the city gathering force as it filled the cathedral until the building echoed with the joy of a people welcoming their future.

'I could not do this without you by my side, Natalia.'

'You could, but I am so glad that I am the one to share that future with you, Kadir.'

They were standing on the now-shadowed balcony, safely hidden from the sight of the stalwart revellers still celebrating in the square beneath them.

'Did you ever think we would be here like this that first time we stood on this balcony together?' she asked him.

'Never,' Kadir admitted, 'but I had much to learn then; much that you have taught me and taught me well.'

'The people of Niroli love you already.'

'I hope so, but they cannot love me anywhere near so much as I love you, and will continue to love you— you and our children, this child and the others I hope will come after her. You are my life, Natalia.'

'And you mine, Kadir.'

Silhouette®

Desire

NEW YORK TIMES BESTSELLING AUTHOR

DIANA PALMER

A brand-new Long, Tall Texans novel

IRON COWBOY

Available March 2008
wherever you buy books.

HARLEQUIN *Presents*

Don't miss the last book
in Lynne Graham's fabulous series!

*The Rich, the Ruthless
and the Really Handsome*

How far will they go to win their wives?

A trilogy by Lynne Graham

Prince Rashad of Bakhar, heir to a desert kingdom;
Leonidas Pallis, scion of one of Greece's leading dynasties
and Sergio Torrente, an impossibly charismatic,
self-made Italian billionaire: three men blessed with power,
wealth and looks— what more can they need? Wives, that's
what…and they'll use whatever means to take them!

THE ITALIAN
BILLIONAIRE'S
PREGNANT BRIDE
Book #2707

Sergio Torrente seduced innocent Kathy for one night
of passion. Months later he sees her, pregnant with his
child, and demands they wed. But Kathy knows his offer
is for a marriage purely of convenience….

**Be sure to look out for more books by favorite
author Lynne Graham, coming soon!**

What do you look for in a guy?

Charisma. Sex appeal. Confidence.
A body to die for. Looks that stand out from
the crowd. Well, look no further—in this
brand-new collection, available in April, you've
just found six guys with all this, and more!
And now that they've met the women in these
novels, there's one thing on everyone's mind....

Nights of Passion

One night is never enough!

The guys know what they want and how they're going
to get it! Don't miss any of these hot stories where
spicy romance and sizzling passion are guaranteed!

Look for these fantastic April titles!

THE TYCOON'S VIRGIN
by Susan Stephens

BEDDED FOR DIAMONDS
by Kelly Hunter

HIS FOR THE TAKING
by Julie Cohen

PURCHASED FOR PLEASURE
by Nicola Marsh

HIS MISTRESS BY ARRANGEMENT
by Natalie Anderson

HER BEDROOM SURRENDER
by Trish Wylie

www.eHarlequin.com

HPP0408

HAPPY
Valentine's Day
from Harlequin and Silhouette!

Special Treat!

Since you love books
as much as we do, we
would like to give you a
special Valentine's Day treat
of romantic and heartwarming reads.

Go to
www.HarlequinSpecialTreat.com
to receive your free online reads from us to you!

Plus there's even more, including fun romance
facts, upcoming news, games, e-cards and more!

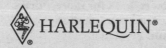

No purchase necessary.

VAL0208